The Peace Weaver

A Collection of Þring Stories

Charles Barnitz

BLOOD AND THUNDER PRESS

Cover by Charles Barnitz and Georgeanne Nelson
Author Photograph by Martha Warner
Illuminated Letters by Karen Hatzigeorgiou

BLOOD AND THUNDER PRESS
3612 Sheffield Lane
Colorado Springs, CO 80907
www.bloodandthunderpress.com

ISBN-10: 1940469236
ISBN-13: 978-1940469232

This one's for James Powell
and Anne McFadgen

CONTENTS

The Peace Weaver

But if there is harm, then you shall pay life for life, eye for eye, tooth for tooth, hand for hand, foot for foot, burn for burn, wound for wound, stripe for stripe.

Exodus 21:23-25

Stanigford and Totmerden
776 AD

Sentwine and Creda, sitting together at the table, stopped talking when I walked into the room, and Creda gestured for me to take a seat at the bench. Rædnoth was standing against the wall with his arms crossed looking up into the network of beams and trusses that supported the roof and the soot-darkened thatch twenty feet overhead. I hesitated, taking in the tableaux, sensing that I wasn't going to like whatever was happening, and then walked over to the table and sat down.

When I'd been a novice at the minster in Eoforwic I'd been called to the novice master's rooms often enough to recognize the lay of this particular bit of land, but I was puzzled because I knew I hadn't done anything wrong or Sentwine would have mentioned it on the spot—surprise meetings with unknown agendas weren't his style. I'd been working for him less than a year, but I knew that much. If he saw a problem he took care of it and moved on, he didn't skulk about.

There was a leather portfolio on the table, fastened by a bit of leather thong twisted around a bone button, and although it wasn't so thick as to give immediate alarm, I knew that whatever was in it was the subject of the meeting.

"How have you been doing, Hring?" Creda asked.

Now I was getting concerned. Creda had been my first master in law, teaching me the essentials about the *dóms* of Elmet as well as Offa's *dóms*, which held precedence over Greater Mercia. I'd trained under him for two winters before he promoted me to assist Sentwine in the *gemót* courts. In those two winters I don't remember him ever asking me how I was doing. Not that he was a cold or distant man, but he was a man who remained focused on the task at hand, which mostly did not include monitoring the health and wellbeing of his subordinates.

"Is there some unpleasantness in my future?" I asked.

Sentwine smiled and looked at Creda. "I told you," he said.

"Told him what?"

"That you would see immediately that—"

"You're in the shite," Rædnoth finished the thought, still looking up into the rafters.

"That you are about to expand your legal education," Sentwine emended with a frown.

I interpreted this exchange to mean that whatever shite I was in Rædnoth was in it too, and that the *geréfa* believed his legal education was already sufficiently broad that he needed no experience like the one to come.

Creda pushed the portfolio across the boards toward me.

"What do you know about the feud between the kindreds of Andhere, who lives in the Stanigford hundred, over close to Hathefield land, and Merewald, who lives in the Totmerden hundred?"

I looked at the portfolio and then back to Creda.

"Only that it exists. Wasn't there a killing a winter ago that never came before the *gemót* because it was part of the feud?"

Elmet is divided into six administrative districts, called hundreds. By law, every hundred meets for a monthly *gemót* court to transact civil and legal business. There are two advocates in Elmet, each with jurisdiction over three of the six hundreds. Because Andhere and Merewald didn't live in Sentwine's jurisdiction, their lethal squabbles weren't my concern. Although I suspected that had changed.

"That's the history of it," Creda said, his eyes flickering down at the portfolio and then back to me.

"What's it to do with us?" I asked, not fooling anyone in the room that the real question wasn't, 'What's it to do with me?'

"Last week Æthelbert of Eoforwic was visiting one of his estates in the Totmerden hundred," Sentwine said, taking up the story. "And he had an unfortunate experience while he was hawking."

Æthelberht was the archbishop of Eoforwic, and I was well acquainted with him. He'd been Alcuin's teacher, and Alcuin had been my teacher, and even though Eoforwic is in Northumbria and the Totmerden hundred is in Elmet, which is part of Greater Mercia, secular dominion has a tendency to be fluidly transitory (whereas the dominion of the Church is rigidly eternal), so the geography of the Church is independent of the geography of the kingdoms, and the Northumbrian diocese of Eoforwic extends well south of the Humber River into Greater Mercia; which explained why Æthelberht was hawking in the Totmerden hundred but not why I was sitting across the table from Sentwine and Creda with a leather portfolio between us.

"What happened?"

Sentwine frowned. "Apparently he was riding after his bird and came upon the body of a man in a meadow in the middle of the *weald*. The body was naked and tied to a post with the man's head spiked on top and his cock sticking out of his mouth. It was clear that he had not died easily."

"Put the archbishop right off his sporting holiday," Rædnoth said.

"The dead man was from Merewald's kindred," Creda said.

"Someone from Andhere's kindred killed him?"

Creda nodded. "That would be our best guess."

I looked at the portfolio again and leaned forward and pulled it closer on the table, but I didn't open it. "And how am I involved in this?"

"Read the history of the feud, and then we'll talk about it."

The feud has existed as an extra-legal remedy for at least a thousand winters, maybe more. It certainly predated the migration of our Anglian and Saxon and Jutish ancestors from the continent, which ancestors, great hairy thugs that they were, kept score by their battle deeds. Honor was everything to them, as it is still to warriors. When there was no war (when the Romans kept to their side of the *limes* and there was no great threat from the nomadic tribes farther to the East) they had to make do with intertribal violence as a way of measuring themselves against one another.

When they sailed across the Frisian Sea to Britannia to fill the void left by the departing legions they discovered that the old political models weren't going to work in their new home, where they were facing Celtic tribes that had been suppressed by Rome for four and a half centuries and now wanted their territory back. They had no supply lines or support systems. They were strangers in a contested country, and as such, they quickly realized that tribal disunity against the well-established and organized Celtic nations meant that they'd be gobbled up piecemeal.

The great warlords imposed their will on the lesser warlords, and individual tribes were eventually welded together into kingdoms that established and enlarged their territories at the expense of the Celts until the Celts, pushed into *Wealas* in the west and *Cornwealas* in the southwest and the land of the Picts in the north, ceased to be the greater threat and the Angles and Saxons and Jutes could turn their attentions to one another. So they finally arrived at a situation where, instead of small skirmishing tribes that lived on opposite sides of a river or a ridgeline, the Cantwara fought the East Saxons, who fought the East Anglians, who fought the Mercians, who fought the West Saxons (and the *Wealsch*), and the Northumbrians did what they do best, which was to fight among themselves when they weren't fighting Picts in the North and everyone else south of the Humber.

And when the borders were more or less stabilized they looked around and discovered that they'd created the very situation they left behind on the continent, except that instead of hundreds of small isolated clans in a sea of oak trees, united only when some greater outside threat forced them to unite, there were now hundreds of kindreds descended from the men who led their tribes from Germania to Britain, living in eight kingdoms on an island with no more available real estate and professing allegiance to whoever was on the throne.

The kings needed men they could depend on to make war against the other kingdoms, but those unfortunate periods of boredom between wars, referred to by everyone who didn't need to define themselves by standing in the shield wall as peace, were devoted to practicing for war, and—as always—the best way to maintain their skills and build a personal reputation was to engage in one of the blood feuds that bubbled along from winter to winter like forgotten stew in a pot.

The feud as an institution is no more or less than the right to wage personal war, but there are rules about how to conduct it. A man's obliged to seek vengeance for injuries to his honor, his family, and his kindred, and if he allows an opportunity to take vengeance pass, he's considered to have betrayed his kindred and himself and becomes a friendless man, liable to penalties for his faithlessness.

On the other hand, there are restrictions as to when and where vengeance can be taken. A man is safe in church or at a public gathering like the *gemót*, and on the road to and from those places provided he doesn't deviate from the path. He's also safe in his home and for the distance of a bowshot from the boundary of his hidage. He can't take vengeance in the presence of the king or the bishop. These stipulations are recorded in the *dóm-bócs* of every kingdom, but limits are often tested or ignored in the heat of the moment. Pressing the feud requires careful premeditation because mistakes can be costly. For example, if the dead man the Archbishop of Eoforwic had discovered had been tied to a post on the archbishop's land, it could be construed to mean in the archbishop's presence, rendering the killing a violation of the rules and, absent the protection of the feud, exposing the killers to a charge of murder and the related penalties.

The blood feud between Merewald's and Andhere's kindreds had been a feature of life in Elmet for three or four generations and had almost achieved institutional respectability.

I looked at Creda and Sentwine and picked up the leather portfolio. "This looks like dry reading," I said. "I'll need to wash it down with a pitcher at the Bitch."

"I'll come with you," Rædnoth said, starting for the door.

The Barking Bitch was an inn just around the corner from the administrative center in Loidis. Creda's men often ate and drank there and the chief advocate kept a running tab that he settled at the end of every month. I reckoned that if he was going to involve me in the adjudication of this blood feud the least he could do was buy me a drink first.

"Do you know what's going on?" I asked Rædnoth as we walked.

8

"I've an idea," the *geréfa* frowned but didn't offer more.

We found our regular table in the corner unoccupied. When the pitcher was between us and the cups were full and I'd had a couple of long swallows to prepare, I opened the portfolio. There were three pages of text and two genealogical diagrams with highlighted fatalities. It came to this:

Andhere was currently the head man of his kindred, which had all its hidage around Stanigford, over in the east, close to the border of Hathefield land, and Merewald was the elder of his kindred, whose hidage was all in the Totmerden hundred in the west. Their great-grandfathers had done business together and had bumped along well enough in the mercantile world of their time until Andhere's great-grandfather decided that one of Andhere's great-aunts ought to marry one of Merewald's great-uncles.

The marriage proposal was turned down, apparently in a tone that Andhere's great-grandfather found insulting. Whoever had compiled the history of the feud was in love with the little details, and he wrote that Merewald's great-grandfather said the girl looked like a "drowned badger's backside." Andhere's great-grandfather responded to the rejection in a manner that Merewald's great-grandfather found equally insulting. According to the history, he said the boy was a "drooling, sheepfocking imbecile" and he'd just been trying to do the other kindred a favor. Feelings were hurt; honor was impugned; trouble was coming.

Because they lived nearly fifty miles apart, trouble took its time. Several winters passed, during which Merewald's great-grandfather might have forgotten about the initial pissoff; at any rate he apparently did nothing more to aggravate the situation. Then someone in Andhere's kindred provoked someone in Merewald's kindred at the solstice festival, gutted him with a short *seax*, and left him to bleed out in the dirt. Before Merewald's kindred could appeal the killing at the *gemót*, Andhere's kindred declared that a state of feud existed between them and would continue to exist until an appropriate apology was made and compensation for their lost honor was tendered.

In the way of these things, there was an initial flurry of assaults, killings, and counterkillings, shedding so much blood so quickly that the charm of it wore off for both kindreds and there was a lull in the opening phase of acute hostility. During that time Archbishop of Eoforwic sent an envoy to talk sense to the combatants, as the Church always does, and the two kindreds refused to listen, as antagonistic kindreds seldom do, and the *witangemót* tried to appeal to their better judgment but found nothing that could be remotely construed as judgment on either side, so no joy there.

Possibly the most rabid instigators of the violence, which is to say the ones who felt the injury to their kindred's honor most keenly (the ones with the smallest cocks), were all killed off in that first virulent exchange—those men are always the loudest and the loudest are always the first to go. Whatever the reason, things calmed down. There were no more killings and the incidence of assault and random beatings tailed off, and several more winters passed before the cycle began again as younger men with equally insignificant cocks achieved positions of influence in each of the kindreds and stirred up trouble again.

To date each kindred had, over four generations, killed a dozen men in the other kindred, broken scores of bones, knocked out numberless teeth, committed a few maimings, one or two blindings and cripplings, and the score now stood even between them. For the past several winters there had been no announced killings, but now the archbishop of Eoforwic had been discomfited by the discovery of the spectacular opening move in a new phase of the blood feud, and he'd complained to the *Ealdorman* of Elmet, who'd decided to intervene, which somehow involved me.

I finished my ale and closed the portfolio. Rædnoth drained his cup and suppressed a burp.

"Let's go see what they want us to do," I said.

A peace-weaver?" Rædnoth snorted. "Really? That's your solution?"

I had to agree with the head *geréfa* on this one. Peace weaving is one of those things that sounds good—one of those things that in theory *ought* to work—but is finally one of those things that almost never comes to much in practice. It usually only leads to grief for the peace-weaver.

A *friðo-webba*, a peace-weaver, is a woman from one feuding kindred (or tribe or nation) who gives herself in marriage to the enemy kindred (or tribe or nation) in an effort to restore harmony and, in a small way, compensate for the men dead in the feud by bearing sons to replace them. It's an elegant metaphor, a poetic kenning—the weaving of a tapestry of peace on the loom of the woman's sacrifice—but as far as those of us on the ground are concerned (which is to say those of us who've seen first-hand the carnage and pain and loss of a blood feud) it's just another inadequate remedy thought up and imposed by old men who are remote from the unintended consequences of their decisions.

Willing or reluctant, a peace-weaver was leaving her kindred to live among people with a history of hatred for her bloodline and who have often sustained personal losses at the hands of her uncles and brothers and cousins, and who are well-positioned to make the rest of her life a sentence of attenuated misery. She can look forward to bearing sons who'll adopt the attitudes of her new kindred toward her old kindred, and who will quite likely take up arms against them, so that maybe her sons will have the pleasure of killing those very brothers and uncles and cousins whose lives she was trying to save by devoting her life to restoring amity.

It would be a lonely existence, isolated

among distrustful people, resisting, as the years passed, the tidal pull of their animosity and the temptation, as she grew more distant from her own kindred, of surrendering to their resentment and dislike and making it her own. For most *friðo-webba*, the best hope of peace they have is the promised peace of the grave.

Very occasionally it worked. Very occasionally the peace-weaver and her husband grew to respect and love one another, very occasionally the peace-weaver had charm and force of personality sufficient to turn old hatreds into, if not new friendships, at least a growing reluctance to seek vengeance for whatever initial insult had started the feud to begin with.

When it had come up in the course of my legal education, it was these rare successes that Creda stressed with disingenuous insistence when I objected to the idea or even expressed lukewarm skepticism on the grounds of logic or common sense. What optimists those old farts in the *witan* are.

Not only was peace weaving seldom successful, it was seldom even attempted because both sides had to agree to weave peace, and the winning side of a feud hardly ever saw the wisdom of calling things off when it enjoyed the momentum of success. Loyalty to the kindred is the greatest loyalty there is; destroying its enemies the greatest duty of everyone in the bloodline.

"I know what you're saying," Sentwine nodded. "I've never seen it work either. It almost always ends in heartbreak for the poor woman, and occasionally she ends up in the *gemót* court showing off her bruises. But what can I say? This has come down from the *ealdorman*. The *witan* put it to both kindreds and let them chew it over for a month, and then Andhere sent word that he agreed and that a woman from his kindred had volunteered."

"Wait, Andhere?" I asked.

"Volunteered?" Rædnoth seemed to have trouble believing the voluntary nature of this woman's agreement.

"That's what he said, and who are we to doubt it?"

Rædnoth shrugged and remained silent. He drummed his fingers on the table and stared off into space. He was clearly not saying something.

"Wasn't it Andhere's kindred that killed the man the archbishop found? Why's he offering a peace-weaver when he's ahead of the game?"

"Maybe he's anticipating some disastrous reprisal," Creda said. "The *ealdorman* doesn't care; he just wants to take advantage of this opportunity."

"And what are we to do?" I said after a moment's resigned silence.

"You and Rædnoth pick up the girl at Andhere's *tún* and escort her across Elmet to Merewald's *tún*. It should only take two days. Deliver her to the church, stay for the ceremony, and come back."

"Have I angered you in some way?" I asked.

"This is an easy assignment, not punishment," Creda said. "Escort duty."

14

"Then why an assistant advocate and a head geréfa? Why not a couple of *your geréfas*? Christ, why doesn't Andhere take her himself?" I looked at Sentwine, but Sentwine had become interested in a stray thread in his cuff and didn't meet my eye.

"Andhere has some concerns about his own safety until peace is actually woven," Creda said. "He's not about to ride onto his enemy's hidage until he thinks it's safe to do so."

I could understand that, especially since someone from his kindred had just beheaded someone from Merewald's kindred and tied the corpse to a post. Things like that tend to make for an uncertain welcome on the *tún* of your new in-laws.

"And we thought that sending you would elevate the importance of the affair," Sentwine added. "We want them to know that we take this seriously."

"When?"

"At the end of the week."

As I explained the nature of the assignment and the misguided futility of the intention behind it, I could see Oswith's sympathy for the girl who'd volunteered to weave peace between the two kin groups grow. Women are often the sacrificial pawns in the politics of marriage, and although it's written into all of the law codes that no one can force a woman to marry someone she doesn't want to marry, that law's ignored as much as observed. Most families don't hesitate to bring their coercive power to bear if they think it will benefit the kindred. Oswith had stopped drawing the wooden wooling cards against each other and gave me all her attention.

Sometimes I'm reluctant to talk to Oswith about the details of my work because she tends to be overly sensitive to the situations I describe, but for that very reason I often give in to the impulse because her more sympathetic perspective often makes me reconsider my initially cynical reaction. I felt bad for the girl, but not in the way Oswith did—I think because Oswith could more easily imagine herself in the situation than I could.

Not that my wife had been coerced into our marriage; we'd both come to it happily and somewhat impatiently, but as a woman she had a more immediate sense of what it might be to find yourself in the position of having to weave peace between two enemy factions.

"What do you think?" I asked when I was done with the story.

Oswith set the wool combs aside and sat up straight on the bench.

"You say the killing's started again. Will this be dangerous?"

"I very much doubt it. Andhere's kindred did the killing, and he's the one offering the peace weaver. Merewald's kindred might be looking for revenge, but they won't take it out on a *geréfa* and an assistant advocate. That would just bring them more trouble when they have too much already."

"What about the girl?"

"You mean is it dangerous for her?"

Oswith nodded.

"Her life's probably ruined," I said. "*That* danger is past at least."

"What does Rædnoth say?"

"Rædnoth's chewing on something, but he hasn't spit it out."

"Is he worried?"

"Seems more irritated than worried. I reckon he thinks the assignment rightly belongs to Ingulf's *hird*, not us. Ingulf sometimes uses his seniority to get out of things he doesn't want to do, and we have to take up the slack."

"But the girl's willing?"

"According to Creda she offered herself up as the peace weaver."

"No matter what Creda says or how the girl appears, she'll be afraid," Oswith told me. "She'll be afraid for her kindred, for any children that might come, but most of all for herself."

I nodded. Our conversation reminded me that the girl wasn't just a package to deliver, however objectively the *witan* might consider her—a mere element in a transaction that would restore order to a part of Elmet that was in disorder.

"The girl's about the same age as Eadgiþ," I said.

My sister Eadgiþ had recently become a nun. Oswith and I had tried unsuccessfully to talk her out of a religious life, but it's almost impossible to talk the women in my family out of anything after they're set on it. I wondered if anyone had tried to talk the girl out of becoming a peace weaver.

"Isn't it strange that the kindred winning the feud wants to stop it?"

"It's unusual," I agreed. Oswith had put her finger on the same odd aspect of the situation that had initially caught my attention. "Creda thinks they might be afraid of a reprisal from Merewald's kindred. Maybe they're weak and don't want it known."

"Then why kill someone and invite revenge?"

"Christ knows," I said. "Every kindred has at least one hotheaded arsehole who acts without thinking.

"Then the girl's a hostage."

"Every *friðo-webba's* a hostage," I said.

"She'll be scared to death."

"What will she be most afraid of?"

"If it were me it would be that my sacrifice meant nothing."

Andhere's hidage was in the boggy ground near the border of the even boggier Hathefield land to the east. The Humber estuary is fed by so many small rivers and streams that no one even remembers what half of them are called, but the largest watercourse is the Trent River, which drains the middle of Mercia into the Humber. The area isn't as pestilential as the Fens, but it's close.

More than half of the economy of the Stanig-ford hundred depends on marsh fishery (birds, fish, reeds, eels). If they could devise a productive use for blood-sucking bugs they'd be the richest area in Greater Mercia.

The Romans had engineered a network of roads there so they could march north and south, or east into Lindsey, so even though the clouds of bloodsuckers in the air make travel uncomfortable, it's efficient and fast and your feet stay dry.

Rædnoth and I are familiar with the three southern hundreds of Elmet because that's our *gemót* court jurisdiction, but neither of us had been to the area by Hathefield land before; it's in Ingulf's jurisdiction. When I asked why Creda didn't assigned Ingulf's assistant Cwichelm to escort the peace weaver across Elmet (presumably he knew the territory because both hundreds were within their circuit) Creda told me that because Rædnoth and I were unknown in the hundred we'd have the kind of authority that attends the unknown, and that it couldn't hurt to wrong foot their expectations. Rædnoth and I both understood that flimsy bit of sophistry to mean that Cwichelm commanded no respect among the members of either kindred and was best left out of things.

The weather was cooperative at least. It was one of those sunny days when even Hathefield land looks congenial, and there was enough of a breeze to discourage all but the most ravenous of the winged insects that haunted the roads in search of food.

The closer we got to Stanigford the higher the water table became, and dry ground agriculture gradually gave way to wetland husbandry. Ploughed furlongs disappeared, upland heath disappeared, forested land disappeared, the world flattened into marsh and reed seas, the sky became immense, and familiar woodland songbirds were replaced by stick-legged waders that preferred eating frogs and fish. We crossed the Don River at the stony ford that gave the village and the hundred their names and rode on without stopping.

We'd gotten exact directions from Ingulf so we could avoid the inconvenience of having to ask directions from the locals, who always seem to think it's a joke to send you out of your way, and half an hour after we left the Roman road for a dirt causeway we rode up to the gates of Andhere's *tún*, located on the highest, driest ground available, which wasn't saying much.

Andhere and his family were waiting for us when we crossed the wooden bridge that led to the open gate of the *tún*; they'd assembled to meet us in front of the hall. Like many *túns* in marshy areas it came with a ready-made moat and there were a few flat-bottomed boats on the bank. The distinguishing feature of the place was a giant willow that looked like a mound of grass from a distance, and there was a long table in its shade.

The men in Andhere's kindred, at least the ones who were there to greet us, were all on the older side, only two or three of them were under 40 winters. I assumed they had sons who were off doing the work (or the murders) but none of them were there to meet us. The crowd seemed to be composed of the heads of families and their wives. It was odd that there were no younger men in evidence. I wondered if that might not be the impetus to weave peace—not enough manpower to carry the feud forward.

My father had once characterized marshland dwellers that lived close to the border of Hathefield land as either stringy sallow types or stringy florid types, in either case given to sweaty, feverish diseases. Andhere seemed more the florid type to me, though not so stringy.

"I'm Hring, assistant to the advocate Sentwine," I said. "This is Rædnoth, Sentwine's head *geréfa*. We're here to escort a daughter of this kindred to her new home."

There were protocols for this sort of thing, but Andhere didn't seem to be aware of them. He skipped the elaborate greeting, gestured for us to dismount, and led us into the shade of the willow, where the table had been set with pitchers and cups and bowls that were covered with overturned tightly-woven baskets to keep the flies off.

Andhere had seen more than 40 winters. He was tall and sturdy looking; he carried himself with the assurance and poise of a man who was foremost in his kindred because he was a competent leader. The fortunes of the birthing order are fickle, so when the oldest son turns out to be the one who's best able to lead the kindred, everyone counts themselves lucky. That's the sort of confidence that clung to Andhere like his smell.

"Did you have an easy trip?" Andhere asked, pouring a cup of ale for me and then for Rædnoth and then one for himself.

"No problems on the road," Rædnoth said.

"We've accommodation for you tonight," Andhere said. "You can get an early start tomorrow and possibly make it the whole way in a long day."

"We've planned a two day trip," I said. "That way we don't have to push hard. You never know what will happen on the road."

"If you're worried that Cenegiða will slow you down, don't be. She isn't one of those women needs a waggon to carry her and pillows to sit on and a servant to feed her sweetmeats and chilled cider. She's as good a rider as I am, and she can stay in the saddle as long as anyone I know; it's like she's part of the horse."

"What's Cenegiða's place in the kindred?"

"She's the daughter of my cousin Wærnoth."

"I'd like to talk to him," I said. I wanted to be able to put Oswith's mind a little at ease about the voluntary aspect of the peace weaving when I told her how the trip had gone. Rædnoth might feel better about it as well.

"So would I," Andhere said. "But he was killed last winter."

"What happened?"

Andhere shrugged. "He just disappeared," he said. "But we've reason to believe that he was murdered by Merewald's kindred. That's why Cenegiða stepped forward to be the peace weaver, so no one else has to live through the loss of a father or a brother or a son."

The feud had been going on so long that no one bothered to claim credit for the killings anymore; each kindred just assumed that any disappearances or mysterious deaths were a result of it. They'd become complacent about their murders. If feuding kindreds stopped claiming responsibility for feud-related killings we ended up wasting time and manpower trying to discover the killer. No wonder the *ealdorman* wanted to stop it.

And the girl's father had been a victim. Though no one spoke of it, the latest killing of someone in Merewald's kindred had probably been a reprisal for that. What could I say? Her motives were pure and had emerged from her grief. I was familiar with extreme reactions to grief, and I could understand why she hoped to be able to save others in her kindred from that experience. Still, I thought it was just another of grief's delusions, just another bad decision made in a despairing moment that would haunt her for the rest of her life.

My own sister Eadgiþ had recently made such a decision, discovering that the man she loved was really just interested in carrying off her maidenhead as a trophy. He was the son of the *ealdorman's* horse *thegn*, and he'd been in determined pursuit of Eadgiþ's cherry for six months when my older brother Tilmund accidentally discovered him in the hay with the daughter of a woodwright in Loidis.

Eadgiþ hadn't taken it well and had removed herself to a convent, heartbroken. She was only just sixteen and at the mercy of her extreme emotions—unwilling to believe anything bad about the horse *thegn's* son when she was in love with him, and then unable to believe that she wouldn't be heartbroken forever when she was out of love with him. Oswith and I tried to talk her out of the convent, but she wouldn't listen to us. Twelve winters younger than we were, I suppose she couldn't imagine that we might have any advice worth listening to. Grief will push you to the limits of understanding.

After we shared the symbolic bite of food and cup of water that meant we were under Andhere's protection, we relaxed in the shade, exchanging pleasantries and helping him drain a pitcher of good ale. Then we went into the long house where the table was set and the rest of the family had gathered. It was a minor feast, and the girl Cenegiða was the guest of honor, feted by her kindred for stepping up to the un-pleasant task ahead of her.

"This is my foster-daughter, Cenegiða," Andhere said when we were in the hall.

Cenegiða was a little bit of a thing, possibly no more than five feet tall; she barely came up to my chin. She glanced up at me and Rædnoth and made a shallow curtsy and then kept her eyes on the floor. She looked even younger than she was, timid and frightened. Oswith had been right about that—Rædnoth and I could both see that she was afraid. Twenty winters

separated her from her next youngest kins-
woman in the room.

"It's a brave thing you're doing," Rædnoth
said.

The girl's neck reddened and she nodded.
She took a deep breath and let it out.

"You can go to your place," Andhere said.
The girl curtseyed again and walked down the
length of the table.

"She's a shy girl," Andhere told us as he
watched her walk away.

I thought about the opening line of "The
Wife's Lament": "I make this song of myself,
deeply sorrowing, my own life's journey."

Although Cenegiða wasn't a great beauty in
the literary tradition of peace weavers like
Wealhþeow, she was attractive in the clear-
eyed, high-breasted, innocent way that a young
woman stepping up to her duty with a weight
of grief on her shoulders sometimes is—a bit
distant as she contemplated the gathering reality of the decision she'd made, no longer theo-
retical now that she could look through the
flames in the hearth fire at the two men who'd
come to deliver her to her doom.

Cenegiða's light brown hair was in wild disorder, a symbol of her freedom and virginal
innocence. Her dress was russet colored and set
off her blue gray eyes. She had symmetrical
features, framed by her hair, that seemed almost beatific in repose, but I got the sense that
in other circumstances she'd likely be warm
and approachable. It was hard not to feel sorry
for her, and I resisted the impulse to take her

aside and try to talk her out of this whole peace weaver business. She reminded me of Eadgiþ, and I knew that my impulse to turn her from her purpose was because I still felt bad that I hadn't been able to turn my sister from hers.

"She's a right honey, isn't she?" Rædnoth whispered, barely loud enough for me to hear the question.

"She is that," I agreed. "What a waste."

Cenegiða sat in a chair at one of the side tables and spoke to a series of men and women who approached her with a deference that, it seemed to me, made her uncomfortable. With small variations, these conversations followed the same pattern. Someone would approach her and then kneel beside her chair. Cenegiða would lean close to the person and they would whisper together for a few moments. Sometimes a small gift would be offered and accepted, never anything that couldn't be transferred from hand to hand—a small bronze balance, scissors, a bone-handled knife, a hand mirror, things of that sort. Then her kinsman or kinswomen would kiss her on the cheek and stand up, perhaps linger for a moment, and then return to their place at the table. They all seemed respectful of the implications of her decision as they said their farewells. Some of the women cried.

"I haven't any experience with peace weaving except what's written in the *dóm-bóc*," Rædnoth said to Andhere, "but isn't it usual to treat it more like a conventional wedding?"

"You have more experience than *I* do,"

Andhere said. "The bans have been posted; Creda composed a marriage contract; there's a morning gift; Merewald's kindred paid the bride price—all of the forms have been observed." He shrugged as if to ask what more Rædnoth wanted. We all knew that the real point was to bring the feud to an end, not plan the perfect wedding.

"It just seems odd to send the girl off with strangers."

"Can you assure my safety?" Andhere asked. We all knew that the recent killing and crass display of the naked, beheaded corpse made that next to impossible. Feeling would be running hot and fierce in Merewald's kindred. In fact, I was surprised that they'd accepted the idea of a peace weaver. In situations like this revenge was generally the first order of business. The *frioðo-wær*, the agreement and covenant of peace that would assure Andhere's safety, did not yet exist. It made me a little concerned for Cenegiða's well-being.

I suppose they could have met in a neutral spot, a church or a royal *tún* where Offa's *frið-borh* applied, and conducted the wedding ceremony there, but Creda told me it had been work enough to get Merewald to agree to the peace weaving at all, and he'd insisted it take place on his home ground.

"What route are you taking?" Andhere asked us, changing the topic.

"We go as far as Wacanfeld tomorrow," Rædnoth said. The village was well sited on a hill with good plough land all around it and close to the Calder River. It was about half way to our destination, south of Loidis, and there was a thick stretch of the Forest of Elmet a little north. It was a *gemót* place and there was a royal *tún* with a *feorm* barn.

Andhere nodded. "I know it," he said. "I once attested to a cattle sale at a *gemót*. It should be easy riding from there until you get into those twisty little valleys in the Totmerden hundred."

The Totmerden hundred was located hard by the great rocky ridge running north to south, where the Pecsætna made their homes in the crenellated little valleys of the eastern drainage that channeled the water from the high ground—narrow and windy and easily defensible.

I looked around the hall and decided that we were intruding.

"This is the last night she's going to have with her kindred," I said to Rædnoth. "Let's leave them to it."

We excused ourselves from the table. Andhere had made a place for us in a smaller guest house not far away, and we went there and into our blankets.

I t was cloudy the next morning when we woke up. I don't know how long the farewell feast had gone on the night before, but the hall had been put to rights by the time we walked in to break our fast before we left the *tún*. Cenegiða was waiting for us together with

Andhere and his wife and several aunts and uncles. The mood was somber. The smells of fresh bread and frying bacon greeted us when we opened the door, always welcome morning smells, and we ate quickly so we could get on the road.

Cenegiða was dressed for riding—leather trousers and a warm wool tunic and hood. In boy's clothing she seemed to be even younger, like a little girl playing dress up in one of her brother's outfits. One by one her older kinsmen and women said goodbye to Cenegiða and left before we'd finished eating.

The grooms had our saddled horses waiting for us outside the door. There was a pack horse that was loaded with two leather chests containing Cenegiða's clothing and the personal property she was taking to the marriage. It seemed a cold sendoff, but I made no comments as Rædnoth and I checked the tightness of the saddle girths and mounted our horses. Cenegiða embraced Andhere and his wife and then the groom boosted her into the saddle and checked the length of the stirrups. When he was finished she brought her heels to the horse's ribs and rode out of the gate without looking back. Rædnoth looped the pack horse's lead through a saddle ring and followed. I went last.

We rode the first hour in silence, and the silence stretched into the second hour. My few attempts to start a conversation with the girl were met with a polite stillness. Andhere had been right about her skill on a horse; she handled her mount better than some of the *geréfas* in Sentwine's *hird*. I wondered if she had brothers who'd taught her, or if her father, in the absence of sons, had given her the attention he would have shown them. She seemed to need the quiet, and I let her have it. It was a dispiriting morning, after all—a young girl leaving her home and family for an uncertain future among her enemies; I couldn't imagine how things could get worse for her. Two hours after we left Andhere's *tún* it started to rain.

We rode into the village of Wentbrycg to discover that the bridge that gave the place its name was under repair and not open for crossing. They were strengthening the trusses and replacing worn decking in fulfillment of their *brycgweorc* duty, and we had to ride a mile upstream to splash across the Went River at a rain-dimpled cattle ford.

As the afternoon progressed, Cenegiða's silence grew into a kind of brittle stoicism, as if she were enduring the ride and the rain and our companionship as lesser inconveniences to be gotten behind her so that she could undertake the greater misery that was going to be her future among Merewald's kindred. I found myself wondering, as I watched her stiff back, what she'd been like before she'd decided to become a peace weaver, before her father had been killed in the feud, before she'd hardened her heart and chosen her fate.

My sister had been a happy girl, laughing through the day, glad in her life, fortunate in her circumstances, and all that had been stolen from her by a horse *thegn's* son with a stiff cock.

It wasn't difficult to imagine that Cenegiða had been the same sort of girl. When she smiled, as I'd observed once or twice last night, she seemed as if she'd never known worry. But as we entered the afternoon she looked as if she'd never known anything *but* worry, as if every step the horse took was a step closer an unpleasant fate, and, because I shared that feeling, I had no words of comfort for her. And yet at the same time she retained a grace and a sort of innocent dignity that I had to admire. Another, more poetic, meaning of *friðo-webba* is "angel," and I had to admit there was something sadly angelic about her.

We stopped at a small croft that belonged to a *thegn* in the district and identified ourselves to the crofter, who was occupied with barn work. He stood in the shelter of a thatched lean-to where there was a small forge and looked at us through the drips, and after a bit of wrangling allowed us to come in out of the rain so we could eat the boiled eggs and salt pork that Andhere's wife had given us for the ride. The crofter was fascinated by Cenegiða's ethereal good looks, and he could barely take his eyes off her until a short, muttered conversation with Rædnoth sent him off to accomplish some suddenly-remembered business in his house.

I laid out the food on a barrel head and we were about to start eating when Cenegiða closed her eyes and bowed her head to pray. Rædnoth and I hesitated, looking at each other. Saying grace was one of those spiritual niceties that had fallen by the wayside when we were riding the *gemót* circuit.

"How much farther are we riding today?" Cenegiða asked us when she'd finished her short prayer. It was the first time she'd spoken to us.

"About as far as we've already come," I told her.

There was a pause and I thought that was the end of the conversation. Until now she'd been determined to stay lost in her own thoughts, barely acknowledging our company. I pinched salt onto the egg and bit into it.

"How did you come to be escorting me to the Totmerden hundred?"

When she spoke she seemed to be numb, the way you sometimes are before you make your peace with the knowledge that something's irrevocably lost. Rædnoth and I exchanged a look. Her tone expressed no real interest. Maybe it had been easier to ignore us when we were riding but now, sitting together over food, her early training about the necessity to be polite was asserting itself almost without her control.

"The *ealdorman* told Creda what he wanted done, and Creda told us," Rædnoth said.

She nodded, considering his answer.

"But I've never seen either of you before. I thought it would be the advocate who attends the hundred *gemót* or his assistant."

"Ingulf had other duties to see to," I said, swallowing.

"Did you ask for this duty?"

"When you work for Creda you take what

duty comes to you. Are we unsatisfactory in some way?"

"Not at all," she smiled distantly. "I was just curious."

"It's an honor for us," Rædnoth said. "I've never met a peace weaver before. It's a brave thing to do."

"The feud has to stop," she said. Her attitude and tone changed as if she were reciting a lesson she'd learned by rote; she seemed almost defiant. "Men think the feud is about fighting and vengeance and honor, but they don't bear the results the same way women do. Most of the time innocent people are killed—just men and women going about their lives whose bad luck it is to be born into a feuding kindred and to be at the wrong place at the wrong time. The men who start the feud never die in it."

"There's rules to carrying out the feud," Rædnoth said. "Women and children are exempt from fighting. Combatants have to declare themselves."

Cenegiða smiled at Rædnoth as if he was simple-minded. The chief *geréfa* of Sentwine's *hird* stopped talking because that smile made him hear what was coming out of his mouth, and no one likes to catch themselves talking nonsense as if they believe it.

We sat listening to the rain patter on the thatched roof of the lean-to. Cenegiða looked at the washed out pasture land and tears made their slow way down her cheeks.

"Is there anything we can do?" I asked.

"Can you promise me that this isn't a mis-

take?" She asked. "Can you tell me that Merewald's kindred won't treat me like a slave? That
my husband won't mistreat me? That my children won't hate me because I was born into a
kindred that was at war with theirs?"

I couldn't make any of those promises to
her, because the things she was so afraid would
happen pretty much matched Rædnoth's and
my expectations point for point. Cenegiða was
more alone at that moment than she'd probably
ever been, and the *geréfa* and I felt that loneli-
ness almost as much as she did because there
was nothing we could do or say that would relieve it.

"Who are you to marry?" I asked.

"Merewald's son, called Ingwald. Do you
know him?"

Her question was freighted with the forlorn
hope that we might have something good to say
about him, that we might be able to give her a
little reassurance that the man to whom she was
about to give over her virginity and the rest of
her life wasn't altogether detestable. It was un-
likely she'd ever seen him, or he her; it was just
an arrangement made for them both by the
heads of their kindreds. She was welcome to
hope all she wanted. We all need hope.

I looked at Rædnoth, who just made a noise
in his throat and looked into the rainy distance,
shaking his head.

"Afraid not," I said.

"What was it made you decide to be the
peace weaver?" Rædnoth asked her. "Did your
family insist, or was it your idea?"

"I have no family," she said. "My mother died five winters ago, and I've no brothers or sisters. When my father disappeared I went to live with Andhere. When the *ealdorman* sent word that he wanted to see peace woven between the kindreds I thought it might be a chance to end the killing."

Rædnoth and I looked at Cenegiða. She had a sweet optimism under that sadness and fear that was probably the only thing she had to hold onto. I found myself wishing that she might be one of the rare few peace weavers who were able to weave a peace that would last. With her parents dead, there was nothing left for her in life but marriage or the convent, and if she had to make a marriage, this was the one that would bring the most benefit to her kindred.

"The rain's letting up a bit," Rædnoth said. "We should get back on the road if we want to reach Wacanfeld by dark."

Wacanfeld sits on a low hill on the north bank of the Calder River, which we crossed at another muddy ford at a little village that boasted a stone chapel and not much else. The royal *ville* and the *feorm* barn are on higher ground to the east of the village proper, well above the seasonal flooding. It was the center of the Wacanfeld hundred, but the *gemót* was two weeks away, and the village was drowsy with routine activity at the end of the ploughing season. The *ville* itself was at reduced levels of staff because the surplus food render had been sent north to Loidis for the *ealdorman's* consumption before it spoiled.

The *tún-geréfa* and his wife were expecting us because Creda had sent word of our coming, and they showed us into the hall, where the cup *thegn* already had food set out and the hearth fire crackling. The prefect and his wife, a short man called Gosbeorht and a taller woman called Wærburh, greeted us warmly and made us welcome with all appropriate courtesy. Wærburh took charge of Cenegiða and showed her to an apartment at the end of the hall, so she could change into dry clothes from one of her leather travel chests. The butler took our cloaks and hoods and strung them on a rope that ran parallel to the hearth, and since neither Rædnoth nor I had a change of clothes, we stood by the fire and let the heat warm us as best it could.

Gosbeorht himself handed us cups of mead and stood by while we toasted our thanks. Because this hundred was also in Ingulf's jurisdiction neither of us knew Gosbeorht, although I recognized him from the times he'd attended the *witangemót* in Loidis.

"How was the road?" he asked.

"Wet and muddy," Rædnoth said.

"The girl?"

"Afraid, but stepping up to her fate," I told him.

"I've never met a peace weaver," the prefect told us, looking over his shoulder toward the room where his wife was helping Cenegiða change clothes.

"She's got a sweet nature," Rædnoth told him. "I was hoping for someone it wasn't as easy to like."

"Why?"

"Because a peace weaver's life is shite," he said.

Gosbeorht sighed. "You're probably right," he said. "We've a daughter her age was married last summer. That was a happier wedding than this one will be."

We stood quietly absorbing the warmth.

"She seems a shy thing," the prefect said after a minute.

"Says her prayers before she eats as well," Rædnoth said, rubbing his hands together and then offering his palms to the fire.

"Speaking of eating, since this is to be her last meal as an unmarried woman I had the cook make a little feast. Roasted a lamb and baked a salmon special for her. The harper's going to play while we eat. I even got into the wine stores. Do you suppose she's ever had wine?"

"Andhere's *tún* didn't look prosperous enough for a wine steward," Rædnoth told him. "Be a treat for her."

By the time Wærburh and Cenegiða returned, Cenegiða in a fresh dress with her hair toweled dry and once more wild down her back, the cup *thegn's* servants were bringing out the food and the harper was playing a low tuning melody at a bench set back from the table.

The hall of a royal hunting *tún* is a big space

because kings always travel with at least a hundred or so retainers or they don't travel at all. They're typically hung with tapestries and decorated with hunting trophies and this one even had a great chandelier suspended from the ceiling with burning oil lamps. We only took up a small corner of one table by the end of the hearth fire, and the rest of the space was shadowy. Cenegiða had never been in a place like it, and she couldn't help but gawk at the bearskins that covered the floor instead of rushes and the tapestries and the glowing chandelier. I watched her eyes follow the rope that held it above our heads—upward to the pulley in the rafters and then along the downward angle to the point where it was secured to a post—as if she couldn't understand the physics of its suspension.

Wærburh kept the conversation moving and away from Cenegiða's impending marriage, and we discussed the hunting that had produced the bearskins underfoot and the antlers affixed to the roof beams and how those fine tapestries were woven in Londinium with such focused attention to detail, showing scenes from the iconography of Offa's dynasty—various warlords and kings and saints and bishops and abbesses. Rædnoth and I were quickly bored hearing about Offa's ancestors and exaggerated family history, but I noticed Rædnoth watching the girl he hadn't wanted to like as she looked around the hall. I wondered if he weren't a little infatuated, not necessarily with Cenegiða but with the *idea* of Cenegiða, possibly wishing he might someday meet such a wholesome young virgin who was not promised to another man. Sadness in a woman made Rædnoth sympathetic.

Rædnoth's responsibilities as the head *geréfa* of Sentwine's *hird* kept him busy on the *gemót* circuit, and while his men might have the occasional free afternoon to go for a walk with a local village girl, Rædnoth was always studying the pending docket so he could plan the next *gemót*, or running errands like this one. He'd never married, and he lived on a small *tún* on his family hidage where he had a few acres under the plough and some crofters to look after it in his absence. I knew he envied my life—Oswith and the children waiting for me in the weeks we weren't on the *gemót* circuit.

Cenegiða had never drunk wine before, and the barrel that the prefect had opened was a good one, sweet and flavorful. It went to her head more rapidly than whatever brackish swill she was used to drinking on Andhere's *tún*, and she started to come out of herself and laughed at Gosbeorht's funny stories. Wærburh remarked that she had a pretty voice and asked her if she would sing us a song. Cenegiða blushed and hesitated, but the harper tried out a new melody, and then another, and finally she recognized what he was playing and sang us a short song, and we all clapped. She did have a good voice.

Happiness, even the hint of its possibility, can seem a cruel joke if you're convinced that it's unattainable.

he rain stopped before sunup, but the ground was still wet and the road was muddy. We got an early start after a breakfast of fresh bread and warm milk and the leftovers from the feast. Wærburh and Cenegiða shared a long embrace at the door of the hall. They seemed to have made a connection the evening before, although it was very possibly based on the fact that Cenegiða's mother was dead and Wærburh's daughter was married and gone and the sad, transient nature of their meeting.

We kept the Calder water on our left and made good time in the river valley, though Cenegiða's mood grew more melancholy as we rode west. We crossed the Calder again at Heptenbryge, below the small market village of Heptenstall, located on the high ground that separates the two valleys at the confluence of the Calder and the beck that runs down from the high ground.

We walked the horses that last couple of miles to draw out the trip as much as we could, although later I wondered if that hadn't just made it more difficult for her. When we came to an open area of the road, and we could see the smoke climbing into the sky above the village of Totmerden, Cenegiða reined in her horse.

"I have to change my clothes," she said. "I can't meet them dressed like this." She indicated her leather trousers and wool tunic and hood and cape.

I looked around and saw that there was a nearby thicket that was dense enough to protect her modesty, and I dismounted and walked to the pack horse. "Which chest do you want?"

"The one on the left," she said, dismounting and leading her horse to the edge of the thicket, where she tied the reins to a branch. As I unfastened the chest, and Rædnoth got out of the saddle and stretched, Cenegiða prowled the edge of the thicket until she found a way inside. She broke some of the branches and folded others into the grasp of the brush and made a passage that I carried the chest into. Six or eight feet in there was a wide area where she could change, and I sat the chest on the ground and returned to the horses.

Rædnoth was letting them crop some grass at the side of the road, holding the reins as he faced them. He looked depressed.

"We're almost finished with this," I said. "Half an hour more and she won't be our responsibility."

"No, she'll be the responsibility of the kindred that wants all her kin dead," he said. "*There's* a happy future."

We stood there waiting while the horses chomped the weeds, and after five minutes we heard her moving through the bushes and she stepped out of the thicket. She was wearing a long gown of tightly woven blue linen with tablet weaving at the hems of the flared sleeves and at her ankles. She had a linen veil over her head that covered her shoulders and the hair falling down her back. I wondered if Merewald's kindred would appreciate the beauty they were getting in this bargain. Rædnoth sighed when he saw her and took a deep breath. I went back into the thicket to retrieve the leather chest.

While I secured it to the pack frame again, Rædnoth boosted Cenegiða into her saddle. The dress was full enough that she could sit astride the horse with her feet in the stirrups. We rode the last half mile down the valley to the village.

Although we hadn't seen anyone on the road they seemed to know we were coming. A group of men and women stood waiting outside the village church as we rode up the street. Some of them were villagers wearing their everyday cloth, who were there out of curiosity, but the wedding party was dressed in their best thread and there was a *mæsse-thegn* wearing vestments in the door of the church. There must have been thirty or more men and women there, the heads of the households that made up the kindred. A man I took to be Merewald was standing beside a younger version of himself, who had to be the son Ingwald. As we got close enough for Ingwald to get a good look at Cenegiða I could see his dour expression change to pleasant surprise. Whatever he'd been dreading, the veiled girl in the linen gown exceeded his expectations.

The village priest stepped out of the church door and moved to stand beside a woman who must have been Merewald's wife and Cenegiða's mother-in-law. She had the stern face of a woman who is about to surrender her son to a woman she's never met from a kindred she hates. Aside from Ingwald's realization that the prospects for his wedding night had taken a turn for the better, it was a cold welcome for Cenegiða. I looked at the assembled representatives of Merewald's kindred and tried to assess their potential for cruelty, and I was disheartened to realize that it was no more or less than anyone's. I realized that, on the strength of two day's acquaintance, Rædnoth and I were the closest thing to a family that Cenegiða had at her wedding.

Rædnoth and I dismounted, and I helped Cenegiða out of the saddle and he led the horses to a post on the edge of the street and tied them on short reins and came back to stand with us. About ten feet separated us from Merewald and his family, and we stood there looking at one another.

"I'm Hring," I said. "Assistant to the advocate Sentwine, and this is Rædnoth his head *geréfa*. This is Cenegiða, the *friðo-webba* from Andhere's kindred, who presents herself to you in marriage to end the bloodshed and the state of feud between your two kindreds."

Merewald and his family took a couple of minutes to examine her as thoroughly as if she were a fertile cow they were buying at the cattle market. Their eyes travelled up and down, lingering on her hips and breasts and face, she stood quietly under their scrutiny with her hands folded demurely in front and her eyes on the ground. At that distance, her face was only a suggestion behind the veil. Her lips moved so faintly that I doubt they could see it from ten feet away, but I knew she was saying a prayer.

"My child," the *mæsse-thegn* said. "Do you undertake this marriage of your own free will and with pure intent."

"I do, father," she said.

"Look at me," the priest told her, and she raised her eyes. A tear rolled down her cheek and she trembled a little. Rædnoth shifted close beside her, brushing her arm.

"Daughter, the responsibility of a peace weaver is a heavy burden to bear. It will be your duty to bring the enmity between your kindreds to an end by being a wife to your husband and a mother to the children you bear him. Merewald's kindred has agreed to receive you into their midst. Do you accept this obligation without reservation?"

"Without reservation or regret," Cenegiða said.

When she said that it occurred to me that the feud had started four generations ago because someone didn't want to marry a woman, and now it was going to end because a woman who didn't want to get married was going to do it despite her fear and reluctance. Like many things in life, the solution was the problem, which was also the solution.

The *mæsse-thegn* looked at Merewald and nodded, and Merewald held out his hand to welcome her into his family. Cenegiða stepped away from us and crossed the little distance to her husband and his mother and father. Merewald and Ingwald stepped apart to make room for her between them, and she took Merewald's right hand in her left, suddenly trapping it against his hip, and her right hand darted into her left sleeve and came out with a blade and with a practiced, economical thrust, she drove it into the left side of Merewald's neck and pulled it forward severing his windpipe and releasing a gout of arterial blood that splashed our legs, ten feet away. She pivoted to her left and used her spinning momentum to shove the blade between Ingwald's fourth and fifth ribs at an upward angle, through his right lung and into his heart. He was dead before the pained surprise could even register on his face. She screamed as she pulled out the knife and ran straight at Rædnoth and me, but we were so shocked by the suddenness of her attack on Merewald and Ingwald that she passed between us before we could react and made it to the horses before we were completely turned around.

Merewald was twitching and pissing himself on the ground with wide-eyed terror, making a horribly wet and ragged sucking sound as he tried to breathe and the air came and went through the gaping hole in his throat. His wife had collapsed between her husband and her son Ingwald, who was laying there staring at the dirt with his dead eyes. The men of the kindred began to react, some of them moving to Merewald, some trying to get to Cenegiða.

Rædnoth, more experienced at reacting to violence, came to himself before I did and he drew his *seax* as he turned. Behind us, Cenegiða hadn't bothered trying to unfasten the reins of her horse, but severed them with a downward slash of the blade and pulled herself into the saddle, dropping the knife to take two fistfuls of mane and wrench the mare's head around. She spread her legs to bring her heels into the horse's ribs just as Rædnoth threw the *seax*, eighteen inches of iron that spun once in transit with a single bright flash of reflected sunlight and hit her in the side like a lightning bolt, point first, disappearing halfway to the hilt into the blue linen of her wedding dress.

She cried out in surprised pain, and her heels convulsed against the horse's side, and the mare bucked forward, unseating Cenegiða as the shock of the wound drained the strength from her fingers and she fell backward over the mare's rump as it bolted and bobbled and then, riderless, slowed to a purposeless walk in the middle of the street.

Cenegiða was crumpled on the ground. She'd landed on the hilt of the *seax* and the impact had driven its length completely through her so the point stuck out of her chest below her right breast. The linen was soaked black with heart's blood, draining into the dirt. Merewald's wife screamed and screamed. Her kindred milled in confusion, leaderless now that Merewald and Ingwald were both dead in the dirt. They stood there helplessly as the *mæssethegn* knelt down and began to anoint the two bodies. Merewald was no longer trying to suck in air; he was lying still with his face in an expanse of bloody mud.

Rædnoth and I walked over to Cenegiða and looked down at her, muddle-headed and numb. Neither of us had yet appreciated what had happened, how we'd been played, or even understood who'd played us. Dead, Cenegiða looked even more afraid and vulnerable than she had in those last few seconds before she'd cut her father-in-law's throat and stabbed her husband-to-be in the heart. She hadn't turned out to be such a good peace weaver, but she knew her business as the angel of death.

The Bean Spoon

If a man commits adultery with another man's wife they shall both be
put to death.

Leviticus 20:10

Loidis, 778 AD

Egbald was a smith in Loidis. His smithy was one of those large, general purpose establishments where they
can fabricate and repair pretty much anything
made of metal, from a belt buckle to a plough-
share. Because his smithy was located on the
main street, which passed through the center of
the town and continued north and south beyond the walls on the course of the old Roman
road, his custom was good; in addition to local
custom he got more than his share of the work
from carters who were doing business in Loidis
on market days and *geréfas* from outlying
hidages who needed more comprehensive service than their local smithy could provide.

48

He had four sons who worked in the smithy, specializing in different aspects of metalwork at different stations around the centrally positioned forge. He'd trained them up himself, and they'd all pitched in together from the time they were able to make a productive contribution, meaning when they were no longer underfoot and had sustained enough minor burns and smashed fingers to understand how to avoid more serious accidents.

My brother Tilhmund is a smith, though his forge isn't as grand or busy as Ecgbald's. He hammers iron in the Scirburn hundred east of Loidis, and most of his steady business has to do with farm implements, but I've been in his forge often enough to be familiar with the layout and the tools and the generally hot and sweaty atmosphere of the place. A working smithy is a din of clangs and hisses and groans, shouted curses, grunts, and the clink and thud of iron, the whoosh of bellows, the stink of scorched metal, and the scrape of shovels in charcoal.

Ecgbald's smithy was quiet at the moment; Ecgbald was taking the day off. In fact, he was taking the rest of his life off. Ecgbald was hanging from a sturdy beam by a length of hemp, black-faced, bloated tongue protruding from his lips, and dead as a holiday ham.

There was a small keg overturned under his booted feet that would have taken his weight if he'd stood on it but, kicked over, left him with eighteen inches of air between his toes and the dirt floor. The front of his trousers was dark and damp from pissing himself. The piss was cold. His body was cold. We could smell that he'd also had a last shite, but I was willing to assume that was also cold without checking it personally.

Wibba had discovered him early that morning when he'd come to see whether the smithy had finished mounting the new guard on his long *seax*. Wibba was shocked, but he was experienced enough to examine the scene without disturbing it, and he'd sent a passerby for Sentwine and me and Rædnoth and stayed there to preserve the integrity of the smithy from the curious and the bereaved.

It looked like a straightforward suicide: a toppled perch from which to take that last long step into infinity, no signs of struggle, no signs of robbery, and no signs of coercion. But because it had happened in Loidis, a block away from the monastery gate and two blocks from the administrative center, we knew we had to at least make a show of investigating.

Sentwine walked around and around the body, his hands clasped behind his back, studying it for any postmortem details that might allow Ecgbald to be buried in the cemetery, because, as a suicide, his mortal remains were headed for an unmarked grave at a crossroad outside the walls and his soul was headed to hell.

"Did you see those scratches on his neck?" I asked.

Sentwine stopped walking and peered up at the dead smith's livid, distended neck. The

scratches on either side of his throat were difficult to see but they were there, more of them
above the rope than below.

"He was trying to pry the noose from
around his throat as his weight tightened it,"
Sentwine said. He tried to lift the smith's right
hand up to look under his fingernails, but the
arm was stiffening and resistant, and the body
started swinging from side to side.

"So he was fighting for his life," I said.

"I've seen a few men who hanged themselves," the advocate said, steadying the body.
"They all had second thoughts as soon as they
stepped off. All of them tried to loosen the
rope, and they all had those scratches. The only
reason an executed man doesn't is because his
hands are tied behind him."

Wibba was standing on the other side of the cold hearth talking to
his squad leader, Mull, and I walked
over to ask him a few questions. Wibba was the
humorist and jokester of the *hird*, and he was
usually only a breath away from a funny quip.
He liked to try out every new advocate joke he
heard on me. One of his more recent was:
"How are an apple and an advocate alike?" To
which the answer was: "They both look good
hanging from a tree." Wibba was quipless at the
moment; finding the smith at the start of his
day had depressed the *geréfa's* mood.

"How long ago did you find him" I asked.

Wibba glanced over to the hanging dead

man and back to me. "The bell for Prime was ringing in the monastery," he said.

"And there was no one about?"

"I passed a couple of people on my way here," he said. "Carters bringing in something or other from the countryside. Also a swineherd and his dog. We can check at the gate to see who came in before Prime."

"But there was no one around here."

Wibba shook his head. "The forge was cold, but the charcoal was laid."

In the warmer months smithies operate at night when it's cooler because the combination of a sweltering day and the heat thrown off by a properly fired forge make for a purgatorial work environment. If Ecgbald had been working last night there would still have been heat in the forge when Wibba found him.

"When did you leave the *seax* for repair?"

"A week ago," he said. "Just before the Barnsleydale *gemót*."

The Barnsleydale *gemót* was fixed for the third week of the month. It was the last of the three monthly *gemóts* in our circuit and our off week followed it.

"Were they expecting you to pick it up today?"

"Ecgbald said a week. Today's a week."

A crowd of gawkers was beginning to assemble in the street. The forge was in the commercial part of town, and men were just coming to work in the shops and warehouses from wherever they'd spent the night. Very few people lived in this area. "Why don't you go encourage the curious to get on with their day," I said, gesturing toward the street.

Wibba nodded and walked away, keeping the forge between himself and the body. The *geréfas* in Sentwine's *hird* were all former soldiers and none of them were squeamish about bodies, but most of the time when they encountered a body it was in a ditch in the countryside where it belonged, not unexpectedly dangling from the ceiling when they were running an errand.

Sentwine and Rædnoth were standing side by side looking up at Ecgbald. I stopped beside them. The three of us stood there watching him sway. I realized that instead of being thrown over the beam and tied off to something solid, the rope had been threaded through a pulley block and was secured to an iron cleat in one of the posts that supported the network of joists that held up the roof of the smithy.

"That's a complicated mechanism," I said.

"They often have to lift great weights, and I reckon it's easier that way."

Much easier. One of the things I'd learned when I studied Geometry at the minster school in Eoforwic is how pulleys work. The cathedral, along with the library and the school and a good part of the monastic cloister, had burned down more than twenty winters before I was born, and archbishops Ecberht and Æthelberht after him had devoted their archepiscopal winters to rebuilding what had been lost. It takes a long time to build a cathedral, especially one large enough to hold 30 altars, and they were still working on it for all the ten winters I was in the minster.

Most of the heavy structural work had been completed before I was born, but there were still work gangs everywhere, and that meant there were engineers who had to ensure that their designs were realized as they'd specified in the plans, and a lot of sweaty *ceorls* with calloused hands hoisting timber and stone with pulley blocks while *thegns* who'd been educated in Gaul supervised and consulted architectural drawings. My Geometry teacher was happy to take us out of the classroom and onto the jobsite so we could get in everyone's way while we observed the application of all those theories about force and vector he'd been reading aloud to us from Hero of Alexandria's book about moving heavy objects.

So a single pulley, which is just a simple wheel to reduce friction on the rope, doesn't really buy you any savings in the amount of force you have to expend—if you want to lift a hundred pounds of weight with a simple pulley you have to apply a hundred pounds of force to do it. But if you add a second wheel and length of rope, you only have to expend fifty pounds of force to lift those hundred pounds. The more ropes and wheels you add, the less energy you expend to lift more weight, with a only little penalty for friction from the wheels.

Another advantage of those years in Eoforwic is that it's a port city, and the docks are full of winches to load and unload cargo from the hulls that come up the tidal Ouse River from the southern kingdoms, and Gaul and Francia, and even farther away. And those winches are all rigged with pulley blocks, so the dock workers can efficiently unload quern stones or hogsheads of ale or crates of bog iron bloom or undressed blocks of stone for minster construction.

I'd spent many a lesson sitting on the Ousebank watching men work those winches while my teacher expounded on the genius of Hero of Alexandria. At the time he'd just seemed like another Greek geometer with too much time on his hands, but I'd come away with an appreciation for how a block and tackle make work easier by amplifying lifting force that I'd put to use when I raised my own *tún* on my own hidage ten winters later.

The pulley in Ecgbald's smithy was like the ones on the docks of Eoforwic. Each block had five wheels in it, so the weight to be lifted was divided by five. If you had to lift 500 pounds off the floor you only had to exert 100 pounds of effort.

"How much do you reckon Ecgbald weighs?"

Rædnoth looked at the smith. "Fifteen stone more or less," he said. "Dead weight."

I grimaced and nodded. "You and Wibba, what a pair of comedians."

To lift Ecgbald, dead or alive, you'd only have to exert about forty pounds of force.

We moved a cart into position and lowered Ecgbald onto the bed and removed the rope from his neck. There was a deep, abraded gouge in the flesh, and there'd been some bleeding where the hemp had torn his skin and from Ecgbald's fingernails. Rædnoth stuffed Ecgbald's tongue back into his mouth and closed his eyes, but the lids wouldn't stay shut, and Ecgbald looked like he was trying to catch one last sleepy look at his forge before he left for the last time.

One of his sons arrived while we were arranging him in the cart, and Sentwine and I held him outside while the *geréfas* worked. By the time they'd covered the body and wheeled it out of the smithy all of his sons had arrived, together with his wife Osilda and two of his daughters. The sons were big and heavily muscled from working in the smithy, but the wife and daughters were small. There was much wailing and weeping and questioning of God's plan. Not for the first time I noticed how people accepted God's plans for everyone else but often opposed His plans for themselves, especially the ones they didn't like.

We separated the family for easier interviewing. Sentwine took Osilda and her daughters aside; Rædnoth and I each took two of the sons. I got the oldest two. The first son was called Baldred, and the second was called Cenbald. They'd been working with their father for years and were the most accomplished of his assistants. Both were in their early thirties and had families of their own.

"Did your father give you any reason to suppose he might do something like this?" I asked.

"It makes no sense," Baldred said. "He was a happy man."

Cenbald nodded in distraught agreement. "Why would he hang himself?"

"So he was in good spirits. No debts? His home life was in good order?"

"No, nothing like that. Men owed *him* money. He's been running this smithy since he took over from his father twenty winters ago. He does the best work in Elmet." Baldred was clearly proud of his father's iron cunning.

"When did you see him last?"

"Early yesterday evening. We were filling an order for horseshoes for the *ealdorman*. Worked at it all day yesterday and half of the day before." Cenbald stepped over to an open wooden box and took out a horseshoe to show me, and then dropped it back with a clank. "When we left he was still organizing the smithy for the next job."

"What's that?"

"A couple of new ploughshares for the monastery," Baldred said. "It will take us a week to make them."

I released the two older brothers to their disbelieving grief. I looked around the smithy again. The place was well organized: the walls were tidily hung with hammers and tongs and lined with work tables. Three anvils were positioned around the forge, which was installed in the center of the smithy with a pair of leather bellows and bins for charcoal and wood. There was a massive work table next to it with a hemp canvas that had been covering the boards pulled off to one side and half onto the dirt floor, exposing gouges and old burns on the surface. Two candles were on their sides, glued to the boards by congealed puddles of wax and a ceramic pot of oil was tipped over, although the stopper had prevented the contents from leaking out. I returned it to an upright position. Tilmund had a table like that for supporting stock that was longer than the forge could accommodate and for dropping small pieces to cool after they went into the water bucket. The rope that would lift a great bloom of bog iron or fifteen stone of strangling smith trailed on the floor where the *geréfas* had left it when they unfastened Ecgbald.

When Sentwine and Rædnoth were done questioning and comforting the dead man's family we came together again beside the forge.

"I don't know what the two of you heard," Rædnoth said, "But I didn't hear a focking thing to make me believe Ecgbald was thinking of suicide."

"It's true," Sentwine nodded. "According to his wife and daughters Ecgbald was a happy man with no more worries in his life than you or me."

"The oldest sons can't believe it, either," I said.

"So we're all agreed then," Sentwine said. "Someone probably murdered the bastard."

There was a glum silence. If we could prove murder, we'd at least ensure that Ecgbald was buried in consecrated ground instead of at a crossroads, but if we wanted to save him from that indignity we needed some suspects.

"The older sons have been with him for years," I said. "Maybe they were getting impatient to inherit. I'll look into it."

Sentwine agreed.

"Rædnoth, talk to the men at the gate," the advocate said. "Market day routines are predictable, so I reckon they know everyone who comes into town early in the morning. They should be able to send you straight to the men they know and maybe identify any strangers for us."

"What are you going to do?" I asked.

"Have breakfast," Sentwine said.

While Sentwine was eating, Rædnoth and I went to the north gate in the town wall. The Roman wall had suffered quite a bit of looting for stone and been restored a number of times, so it was a patchwork of masonry and timber, but the gates were in working order, and they were closed every night and opened again at the start of every day.

We weren't hopeful that we were going to learn anything from the guards. The body had hung there all night and was motionless when Wibba found it, so I was certain that no one had come into the city early and stopped in at the smithy long enough to string up the smith with his own block and tackle.

The *geréfas* at the gate were there as toll collectors and porters more than guards. There were four *geréfas* in the detail, operating out of a small tollhouse where they stayed when it was raining. There was a wicker animal pen beside it and a cess pit. The *geréfa* in charge was leaning back against the wall on a folding stool while his subordinates inspected the contents of a waggon that they'd stopped at the gate. The livestock pen was occupied this morning by two shoats, a lamb, and three chickens, and none of them looked happy about it. It sounded like the beginning of one of Wibba's jokes with an innkeeper as the straight man.

Rædnoth went directly to the man on the stool.

"Busy morning, Osdred?" Rædnoth asked as we approached.

"No more than usual," Osdred leaned forward and tipped the stool's front legs onto the ground. "What brings you into my little corner of the world?"

"Asking questions," Rædnoth said. "You know Hring?"

The *geréfa* nodded at me. We'd never met, but we'd seen each other around. I nodded back.

"What questions could an assistant advocate for the southern hundreds and the chief *geréfa* of his *hird* have for a poor *tol- geréfa*?"

The *geréfa's* attitude was friendly enough in the bantering way of an acquaintance, and I didn't detect an edge to it.

"Don't sell yourself short," Rædnoth laughed. "I bet you know the answers without having to study."

"Let's hear the questions."

"What time did you open the gate this morning?"

"Before Prime, same as every morning," he said.

"Was there a queue waiting to get in?"

"I'd hardly call it a queue," he said. "A shepherd, a swineherd, a couple of thatcher's waggons. The usual."

I glanced over to the animal pen. "Where'd the chickens come from?"

The toll for passing the gate for commercial purposes might be assessed in coin if the merchant was especially prosperous, but more often was assessed in kind, which explained the lamb and the shoats.

"An egg seller," Osdred told us.

"They all regulars?"

The *tol-geréfa* nodded. "What's the trouble?"

"You know Ecgbald the smith?"

Osdred nodded again.

"One of my men found him hanging beside his forge this morning," Rædnoth said. "We thought we'd ask if any strangers came into the city today."

"Not through this gate."

"Would the egg seller, the shepherd, or the swineherd have any business with the smith?"

"I suppose it's possible," the *tol-geréfa* said. "But I doubt it. You can ask them if you want. They'll be in the market." He paused and then looked off in the direction of the smithy. "You think he was murdered?"

"It looks like he killed himself," I said. "We're just making a half-hearted effort to get him buried in holy ground."

"That's the kind of service the citizens of Loidis should be able to expect from their *geréfas*," Osdred smiled at us.

Osdred had been a *geréfa* for about five winters. I didn't know him, but I knew about him; when I'd been Creda's assistant he'd come up before the disciplinary board seven times. I'd only been Creda's assistant for two years. Osdred wasn't a disciplinary problem as such; he wasn't insubordinate or incompetent or dangerous. He was a fockup. One of his guest appearances before the disciplinary board had been for a prank that had gone wrong and resulted in a *thegn* on the *witan* being thrown off his horse into the muddy street; a second had been for accidentally starting a fire that reduced three thatched market stalls to sooty smudges; a third had been for failing to fasten a butcher's gate (something every farm boy learns at the age of three) and releasing a drift of pigs into the shambles before the butcher could stop them.

The pigs, their snouts full of the panicked terminal smells of every pig that preceded them on the road to becoming pork, scattered in a stampede of oinks and squeals, and the *geréfas* had spent the rest of the day running them down. During their brief stay of execution the pigs had trampled and uprooted ten or fifteen garden patches, broken down flimsy fencing, wallowed in street puddles, and menaced a couple of nuns on their way to the almshouse.

Osdred's other four transgressions were in the nature of public lewdness. Osdred was a strapping man with all a strapping man's urges but none of what might be considered a smart strapping man's discretion or common sense. Twice he had been discovered with a woman's legs around his middle—once in the back of a stall in the market and once in a hayloft in a stable—and twice he had been apprehended in alleys bending women over convenient supports (a barrel and the wicker privacy fence around a cess pit). On all these occasions the women had been moaning with sexual transport and refused to prefer any charges against him. On all these occasions Osdred had been caught in the act by fellow *geréfas* and not irate husbands, brothers, fathers, or, heaven forefend, *masse-thegns*, so news of his transgressions could be suppressed.

Each time he was threatened with expulsion from the *geréfas*, and each time he was shifted to another duty squad, and each time he was as contrite as a man caught with his eel in the trap could possibly be. Now he was assigned to the tollhouse at the north gate of the town, were they must have thought there was nothing he could possibly make a hash of.

"Ecgbald was a good sort," the *geréfa* said. "I used to see his spoons here and there before his wife figured it out."

"What does that mean?" I asked.

The *geréfa* looked at me and then looked at the ground and then back in the direction of the smithy. "I don't like to talk ill of the dead," he said.

Rædnoth had turned away, but now he stepped back to Osdred and clasped his hands behind his back in that way of his that meant he was prepared to stand there all day until he heard what he wanted to hear. His head was cocked to the left and his eyebrows were raised expectantly. "Yes?"

Osdred sighed and spat and ran his hand through his hair. I hoped that was his entire catalogue of delaying mannerisms; it was getting hot standing there in the morning sun.

"Ecgbald sometimes met women in the smithy after he closed up for the day," he said. "Some women like a man all sweaty with big muscles. You know the kind I mean."

I did know the kind he meant. Some women like to indulge their fantastical inner lives with a working man who'll mount them with the *ceorlish* enthusiasm of a post rider bringing news of a great victory, and afterward they can drop their skirts down around their ankles and get on with their day. No need to try to make conversation or nag him to take out the garbage or be embarrassed by his crude ways at a feast. Mostly these women were *thegns* who were either married to inattentive husbands, not married at all and without prospects, or widows who had acquired the taste but lacked the opportunity. Some of them had the thatcher around to repair a nonexistent leak in the roof when they were home alone; some of them spent long hours helping the carpenter design a new addition to the weaving house; some of them had the weller out once a month to un-clog the source of the drinking water. Some of them, apparently, made late night visits to the smithy.

"What about the spoons?" I asked.

"Whenever he topped a woman he gave her a spoon," the geréfa said. "Something to re-member him by I suppose."

Spoons were one of the basic products of a forge: easy to make and widely needed. Every-one had a spoon.

"So were these spoons somehow special?"

"Just little spoons," Osdred shrugged. "Three twists and a loop. About as long as your middle finger."

I could picture the spoons. Twisting the hot iron so the shaft of the spoon was a spiral was an easy and basic decorative flourish, and bending the end of the shaft into a loop for hanging it on a nail or tying a bit of leather to it was just as common.

"So he gave his women iron spoons," I said, shaking my head. As a keepsake for a romantic tryst it seemed to lack something.

"Not iron," the geréfa said. "Molded pewter. All smooth and shiny."

"What do you mean his wife figured it out?"

"Last year there was a big row when the wife went after a woman in the market. The woman had one of the spoons around her neck, and the wife must have recognized the work. Maybe Ecgbald gave her one like it when they were courting. Who knows? He was kind of sentimental for a smith."

"You seem to know a lot about him," I said.

The *geréfa* looked sheepish. "We had sort of an understanding," he said. "I used to patrol that street at night, and sometimes I could hear him in there raising a racket. The first time I looked in he was humping away on a work table, and he didn't even hear me until the woman opened her eyes and saw me over his shoulder. Let out a scream," Osdred laughed in spite of himself. "Scared the shite out of both of us." He smiled and shook his head at the pleasant memory that had probably bonded him and the smith.

"What understanding?" Rædnoth asked.

"Oh, well, sometimes he let me use the smithy myself. More privacy."

That explained why Osdred hadn't come before the discipline board again for reckless fornication—he had a place to take his women now.

"And in return?"

"In return I didn't make a stink about Ecgbald entertaining after curfew."

Just two quiff hounds reaching an agreement.

The punishment for a woman caught in adultery was mutilation, and I wondered how many of the women who got a pass from the *geréfa* might be grateful enough to drizzle some honey on his oatcakes in return.

That opens up some possibilities," Rædnoth said as we walked away from the toll house.

He was right. It wasn't a stretch to think that a husband had discovered his wife's indiscretion, or a father his daughter's, or a brother his sister's, and taken his revenge. If apprehended in the adulterous act, the law said that a husband could kill the man without penalty, but like all other judicially sanctioned killings, such as taking a thief or rapist in the act, it had to be announced and proven with evidence. Not generally an issue with thieves and rapists but sometimes more difficult with an adulterer.

"We've got to ask around," I said. "Someone might have heard something last night, or seen something."

"It would also be helpful to know what the spoon looks like."

We went back to the smithy, which Sentwine had closed and locked for the day and set Osgard, one of his *geréfas,* to guard the door. The smithy was unnaturally quiet. I could see dust motes swirl in a sunbeam that angled through the open window as Rædnoth walked across the open area to a cabinet. I looked around at the workbenches and spotted a chest, and I went over and opened it, but all it had inside were some calipers and other measuring tools. There were crucibles and molds arranged on a shelf. Behind me I could hear the squeak of wooden drawers drawn back on waxed runners. I was about to lift the lid on another chest when Rædnoth called out, "Got it."

I walked across the smithy and looked down into the drawer that the *geréfa* was holding open.

"What an optimist," I said.

Arrayed on a cloth were seven pewter spoons as described by Osdred—three twists and a loop—polished and shining in the morning light.

Rædnoth picked up one of the spoons and examined it in the sunlight by the window. "What's this for?" he wondered.

I wondered that myself. The bowl of the spoon was only a little bigger than my little fingernail, teardrop shaped, and shallow. What was its purpose—merely ornamental? I looked around the work tables and found a gather of leather thongs about as long as my leg and I stripped two out of the bunch and threaded the end of one of them through the loop at the end of the spoon handle. I tossed the other one to Rædnoth.

"Better take one so we can split up if we need to," I said,

Rædnoth removed a second spoon from the drawer and then slid it closed. We both looped the thongs over our heads and left the smithy.

Outside, the *geréfa* Osgard was in conversation with a monk. That's somewhat inaccurate; the monk was in Osgard's face with a vehemence and sense of purpose that had backed the *geréfa* up against the wall of the smithy and left him no way of escape.

"What's the problem, father?" Rædnoth

asked.

The monk pulled his attention away from Osgard and rounded on Rædnoth with his features twisted up in anger.

"Who are you?" the monk demanded.

"I'm this man's superior officer," Rædnoth told him. "Has he given some offense?"

"He won't let me into the smithy."

"The smithy's closed today," I told the monk.

"But I have business with Ecgbald," he said. "He's expecting me."

"Ecgbald's no longer doing business here," Rædnoth said.

The monk looked at the solid structure, then noticed that there was no smoke billowing out of the smoke hole over the forge, and only then noticed the absence of the infernal noise that emanates from a working smithy. "What do you mean?"

"He means Ecgbald's dead," I said. "Who are you?"

"I'm Eoric," he said. "I'm the cellarer's assistant at the monastery."

"You're here about the ploughshares," I said, remembering the next job that Ecgbald's son had told me about.

"That's right," the monk said.

"You're going to have to go to another smithy if you're on a schedule," I told him. "Or wait until Ecgbald's sons fire the forge again."

"How long will that be?"

"I reckon after they bury Ecgbald," I said. "Two or three days."

69

"What happened to him?"

Rædnoth and I exchanged a look. "We're not certain," I said. "We're still looking into it."

The monk looked at us and then turned and walked down the street toward the monastery without another word.

Not many people lived in the vicinity of the smithy, the district being predominantly commercial and industrial, but although the street was occupied by a tannery, a barrel maker, a kiln, and a saw mill in addition to the smithy, and a few smaller establishments given over to the fabrication of wood, there were three houses within a hundred yards. They all had garden patches and fenced areas for a few pigs or goats and coops for chickens. They all had dogs that barked when we approached. Rædnoth slipped his hawthorn truncheon out of his belt in case the dogs were so territorial that they'd attack.

The men were gone from all three houses, off at work, but their wives were at home and they were all curious about the activity, or lack of it, at the smithy. No smoke coming out of the roof hole was an obvious clue that the forge was cold.

Our questions were the same at all three places. Did you hear anything from the smithy after sundown last night? Did you see anyone who didn't belong at the smithy last night? Was there anything unusual in the neighborhood the previous evening?

Two of the women answered, "No, no, and no."

The third woman, whose house was closest to the smithy, was more talkative. She'd survived about five more than forty winters, and she appreciated a little excitement in her life. Her husband operated the saw mill in the street, on the other side of the smithy, and her children were grown—the daughters married off and the sons at work with their father. She was home alone and bored and looking for an excuse to put off milking the goat. Often the most productive kind of witness. Her name was Wilgiva.

"Ecgbald's dead," she told us when we asked her if there was anything strange at the smithy.

"How do you know?" I asked.

"My husband found out when he went to the saw mill this morning and he sent our son back to tell me."

"Why?"

"I'm here by myself during the day. He wanted to warn me."

"Did you hear anything unusual last night?"

"Yes," she said. "Silence."

"The forge was cold last night," Rædnoth said, misunderstanding her. "They finished a big job yesterday and they were to start another this morning."

I misunderstood her too. I thought she meant she hadn't heard the usual banging and clanging of a working smithy.

"I know," she said. "Sometimes it's noisiest when the forge is cold."

"What do you mean?"

She plunged ahead without any of the sanctimonious hesitation that we'd gotten from the *tol-geréfa*. Apparently she had no qualms about speaking ill of the dead. "His women," she said. "On a quiet night you can hear them shrieking all the way across the field."

An open space of about fifty rods separated the smithy from her front door.

"Shrieking? Did he mistreat women in the forge?"

"It didn't sound like mistreatment to me," she laughed.

Well. We were talking in her doorway, and I had a quick glance over her shoulder to see if I could spot one of the pewter spoons hanging on the wall, but nothing shiny caught my eye.

"How often did that happen?" Rædnoth asked, trying to keep his tone professional, although I knew him well enough to know he was struggling to keep from laughing.

"Whenever the forge was cold the smith was hot," Wilgiva winked and made a lewd face.

Rædnoth couldn't control it then, and he turned away and snorted.

"You think I'm a vulgar woman," Wilgiva said. "You think I'm brazen and speaking plainly to make you uncomfortable, but that's just the way things were at the smithy."

"Did his family know?"

Wilgiva shrugged. "I heard there was some big disturbance in the market last year when his wife attacked a woman, but they must have composed it without going before the *gemót* because I never heard anything else."

"And it had to do with what went on at the smithy when the forge was cold?"

"I don't know that for sure," Wilgiva shook her head. "I just put two and two together."

The mathematical skills of witnesses were frequently based on the faulty premise that the sum of one odd event plus a different odd event inevitably equaled a set of two connected odd events, so I knew I couldn't automatically accept her conclusion as gospel, but in this instance, supported by the speculation of the *tolgeréfa*, I thought it just might be true.

"How many times did it happen?"

"How many Fridays are there in a year?"

"Every week?"

"Nearly," she said.

"Always the same woman?" Rædnoth asked.

"Now how would I know that?"

"Always the same shrieks?" I rephrased the question for her.

She shook her head. "It's not like I listened all the time," she said.

I had profound doubts about that. I could easily imagine her and her husband pulling up stools in the threshold yard and drinking ale while they made bawdy jokes comparing Ecgbald's current and past performances as measured by the yodels of female delight that carried across the field.

"Have a guess," I prompted.

"Not always the same woman," she said. "I reckon five or six different women over the months."

"But there were no shrieks last night?"

"I didn't say that," she said. "I said I heard silence."

"Well it couldn't have been both, could it?" Rædnoth was starting to lose patience with Wilgiva's narrative style.

"Started out the same as always. Then she really went crazy, screaming like the top of her head was coming off, then it got quiet. That was it. Usually the smith and his women are good for an hour or two of wailing, but last night they were done after five minutes."

I shook my head. Ecgbald must have been a cocksman of prodigious stamina and remarkable luck if he was able to juggle half a dozen women in addition to his wife and mostly keep them apart. There was a small sorority of women in Loidis whose symbol was a shiny pewter spoon. I pulled at the leather thong around my neck and withdrew the spoon from my tunic.

"Ever seen one of these before?" I asked.

She shook her head in the negative. "Awfully small for a spoon," she said.

τ was midmorning and I was getting hungry, but I'd started out to have a follow-up interview with the older sons to decide whether they'd been impatient for their father's holding and hurried him along to his eternal reward, and I'd been diverted by the information we'd gotten from the *tol-geréfa*. I thought I'd better question the sons again before I took a break for a late breakfast.

Ecgbald lived away from the smithy, which had probably kept his wife happily ignorant of his extramural affairs for the whole of his married life. It was unsavory, and the church railed against it, but in fact a married man with a mistress (although in this case six that we knew of) wasn't that uncommon.

The penalties for adultery varied by gender and depended on the social and marital status of the two adulterers. An unmarried woman who was discreet and independent, say a widow or a spinster without male relations, could carry on her affairs more safely than a married woman or an unmarried woman who still lived with her family, but if an affair was exposed she could still look forward to having her nose and possibly her ears sliced off and then nailed to her door until they rotted away or the ravens carried them off. For a man: possibly a fine, possibly a beating. Nothing more unless he was apprehended in the act by a husband or male relative, in which case he might suddenly discover himself and the woman underneath him pinned to the bed by a length of pattern-welded iron.

If the husband of whichever woman in Ecgbald's rotation had been scheduled for a sweaty, big-muscled boffing last night caught them in the act and killed the smith, all he had to do was announce the killing and he was out of jeopardy. I wondered if anyone had presented himself at Creda's door this morning with such an announcement, and I thought maybe I ought to check and save myself some legwork, but we were closer to Ecgbald's house than to the administrative building in the center of town, so Rædnoth and I trudged on.

Ecgbald lived on an acre of land on the other side of town. There were three houses on the property and some smaller sheds and a little stable where a single donkey stood swishing its tail as it watched us walk up to the door. There were five tall elm trees shading the houses and threshold yards. As the most sought-after smith in Loidis, Ecgbald had set himself up on a good property in a good part of town; far enough away from the smithy so the delighted shrieks of his after-hours customers wouldn't disturb the domestic tranquility of the neighborhood.

I knocked at the door with the side of my fist and waited. There was a well nearby, and I noticed the pulley mechanism that would raise and lower the bucket was another of those robust blocks that would make it easy to lift the weight.

The door opened and Baldred, the oldest son, stood in the frame.

"What do you want?" he asked.

Behind him I could hear women crying. The cart that we'd lowered his father's body into was sitting off to one side of the door, so I reckoned they'd brought him back here to prepare the body for burial. Whether the priest would come and anoint the corpse and allow it to be interred in consecrated earth was another matter, and beyond our official remit. For the moment we were only interested in who'd killed Ecgbald, not what happened to him afterward.

"There are some other questions we'd like to ask," Rædnoth told him. "Won't take long."

"Let's talk outside," Baldred stepped into the threshold yard and closed the door.

We walked to a table and benches under one of the elm trees and sat down. The sun was high in the sky, and we were in a wide pool of shade.

"How long have you worked with your father at the smithy?" I asked.

"Since I got my iron," he said. He meant since he'd reached his majority and received the *seax* he carried when he did his *fyrd* service. "So, twenty winters now."

That made him about thirty five winters old.

"That's a long time to be taking orders from your father," Rædnoth said with the air of a man who'd been happy to stop taking orders from his father as soon as he could arrange it.

"Ecgbald wasn't so bad," he said. "He was a good smith and a good teacher. He'd been doing it a long time. When he was young he'd even worked in Gaul for a while, learning what they knew about the craft over there."

"He wasn't hard to work with? Fathers sometimes are, especially if they have high standards." I watched him closely, but nothing in his expression betrayed a murderous impulse when we discussed his father. Still, the deed was done now, so the anger might be dispelled.

"He had high standards," Baldred agreed. "He was a master craftsman. And if you made a stupid mistake he was quick to let you know, but it's been a long time since Cenbald and me made stupid mistakes."

"What about your two younger brothers?"

"What, Eobald and Baldric? They're past making stupid mistake too." He paused and looked at us, catching the drift of our questions.

"You think we killed Ecgbald?"

I shrugged. "We always have questions we have to ask," I said. "You said yourself he wasn't the kind of man to hang himself."

The door opened and his brother Cenbald came out of the house to see where Baldred had gone. Baldred waved him over to the table.

He closed the door on the sound of the women crying in the house and came over to join us.

"What's the matter?" he asked.

"They think we killed Ecgbald," his older brother said.

"What? Why would we kill our father?"

"To inherit the smithy?" Rædnoth asked.

"We loved Ecgbald," he said. "He taught us everything we know."

"Well he either killed himself or someone killed him. We have to decide which it is before long or the priest will plant him at the crossroads and send his soul to hell."

"He didn't kill himself," Cenbald said firmly. "And we didn't kill him. We were here all last night and our wives will swear to it."

"Who would have wanted to kill him?" Baldred asked. "He was an honest smith who never cheated anyone."

"As to that," Rædnoth said. "Maybe it was the husband of one of the women he was shagging when the forge was cold. Possibly the husband of the one he met last night."

The brothers looked startled, and then they quickly reassembled their defenses and closed ranks to protect their father's reputation.

"He never," Baldred said huffily.

"That's a slander," Cenbald grunted. "I'll appeal anyone who says so."

"Come off it," Rædnoth said, pulling the leather thong out of the top of his tunic and dangling the pewter spoon in front of the brothers. "There's at least half a dozen of these that we know of round the necks of Ecgbald's jades."

The brothers watched the shiny spoon swing at the end of the leather as if they'd just seen a baffling magic trick they couldn't explain. We let them stew in silence while we studied their faces. Nothing but surprise.

"So what have you got to say now? Want to help us catch the killer, or would you rather we appeal you for the murder?"

"There were no husbands," Baldred said.

"We have witnesses who heard your father curling women's toes whenever the forge was cold," I told him. "And we know he gave one of these spoons to whoever he topped."

"There were no husbands," Cenbald insisted. "They were all widows."

He glanced back at the closed door of the house and then looked at the weathered boards of the table top.

"Was he crazy? Couldn't he keep it in his trousers?" Rædnoth spun the spoon in a circle in front of them. "Why did he give them spoons?"

"They're bean spoons," Baldred said.

Rædnoth caught the whirling pewter spoon and held it up. "Bean spoons? What, are you supposed to eat one bean at a time?"

"That's the idea," Baldred said. Cenbald snorted out a laugh in spite of himself.

"What are you laughing about?" I asked. "This isn't funny." I hate it when an interview goes off the track like that.

"It's a spoon for the bean," Baldred said. "You know, the bean?"

"The bean," Rædnoth repeated.

"The bean," Baldred said. "The love button, the sugar plum."

Rædnoth looked at them blankly.

"The mouse in the wheat field?" Cenbald prompted. "The pink pearl?"

The brothers looked at us as if we were idiots.

"Don't tell me you two have never gone pearl diving," Baldred said. "Aren't you married?"

Then I understood what he was talking about, but I was still lost, although at least now I knew what part of the wheat field I was lost in.

"Look," Baldred said impatiently, taking the spoon from Rædnoth's hand. He held up the little finger on his left hand and slipped the middle finger of his right hand through the loop in the end of the spoon handle. Then he rested the spoon on his thumb with his forefinger on top of the shaft and put the bowl of the spoon on the tip of his upraised left little finger.

"You dip the spoon in olive oil and put the spoon on the woman's bean," he said. "Then you move it around slow. They go insane. Can't help themselves. Lose all control. He learned about it in Gaul when he was a young man."

Rædnoth's eyes widened, and his face got red as he realized what he'd been wearing around his neck for most of the morning. It took a great effort for him not to pull the loop of leather over his head and throw it away. I bit the inside of my mouth so I wouldn't laugh. Laughing would not be a good thing at this particular moment. Trust the Gauls to invent something to perform an action that you could easily do with your thumb.

"So you knew about your father's women friends," I said.

The brothers shifted their attention to me and Rædnoth slowly took the little pewter spoon from Baldred's hand and laid it on the table.

"He was our father," Cenbald said.

"They were widows," Baldred said.

Together they seemed to think that these two statements covered the topic as comprehensively as it needed covering.

"Who was he with last night?"

"Last night was Brictinda," Cenbald said.

"And so far as you know he met her?"

"So far as we know." Cenbald nodded.

"Who's Brictinda?" Rædnoth asked.

"She lives out of town," Baldred said. "Comes in once a month for the market and meets Ecgbald in the evening then goes home the next day. Her hidage is a few miles west. Her husband was a swine lord, had great numbers of pigs because the hidage abuts a length of the great oak forest. Pigs fatten up on the acorns and then get turned into salt pork for the *fyrd* and the *gesith*. He had a contract with the *ealdorman*, and when he died Brictinda renewed it, so she's well off and independent."

"Children?"

"Grown and married."

I looked at Rædnoth. "We have to send someone out to her hidage to make certain she's alive," I said.

"Why wouldn't she be?" Cenbald was puzzled.

"Suppose whoever killed your father came on them together?"

"Then why wasn't her body in the smithy?" Baldred asked.

"That's a good question," I said. "And when we talk to her I'm sure we'll get a good answer."

The door opened and one of the younger brothers stuck his head out.

"What is it Eobald?" Baldred called out.

"Mother wants to know what's keeping you."

"We'll be inside in a minute," Cenbald told him.

"Do you have to talk about this to mother?" Baldred asked.

"We heard there was some trouble last summer," I said.

"She saw a woman wearing a spoon in the market and lost her mind," Baldred grimaced.

"You mean she knows about the spoon?"

"They were married for thirty five winters," Baldred said. "They got married right after he came back from Gaul. Of course she knows about the spoon. I reckon she knows first-hand."

His younger brother Cenbald shook his head, as if that image might be a little difficult to banish from his mind's eye.

"There's no telling how a local girl will react to the things they get up to in Gaul." Rædnoth said.

"She wasn't a local girl," Baldred said. "Osilda's from Seletún."

"Seletún?"

"Ecgbald met her there when he was apprenticing to his father. They used to get bog iron from Frisia and they picked it up in Seletún. The monks at the monastery there have a wharf where they unload goods before the ships go upriver. That way you don't have to go all the way to Eoforwic."

Seletún was shipbuilding village on the Ouse. There was a wharf there for offloading small shipments for local distribution.

"What did her people do?"

"Worked at the wharf. That's how they met."

"Let's go in and pay our respects," I said to Rædnoth.

There was a lot of iron inside Ecgbald's house, as you'd expect in a place where a smith lived. It was conspicuously displayed: candle holders spiked into the beams, an elaborate cooking rack and tripod and two cauldrons suspended from the beams over the hearth on a track so they would slide over the heat to bring the contents to a boil or off to the side to keep the contents warm. The corners of the table were reinforced with iron straps, and so were the corners of the sleeping benches. The hinges of the door were iron, not leather, and the bolt was an elaborate bit of smithy as thick as my wrist.

Ecgbald was lying on a table at the head of the hearth so they had light to work as they washed the body and dressed him in his best clothes. There was a bucket of dark water beside the table, indicating that they'd had at least a whole day's soot to remove. Maybe all we needed to do was walk around and look for widows with sooty handprints on their asses to discover how many women the smith had been servicing after hours.

The new widow was sitting with her daughters and daughters-in-law, who were trying to comfort her. The two younger sons were keeping a vigil at their father's feet. Two candles were burning in iron holders on either side of Ecgbald's head. His swollen tongue was out of sight in his mouth but his eyes were still partially open, as if he were curious about who would come to his funeral. The abrasions on his neck were hidden by the fabric of his hood, which was pillowed under his head.

I wanted to make this a short visitation so we could get on the road to Brictinda's *tún*, somewhere to the west of Loidis. I hoped we would find her there and not a lot of servants worrying because their mistress hadn't come back from her monthly excursion into town.

Rædnoth and I stood with our heads bowed, saying a *Pater Noster* for the old satyr. He was fiddling with the spoon in his hand, bunched in the tangle of leather. He hadn't been able to bring himself to put it back around his neck. He was more squeamish than I would have expected. As for me, a minster-raised professional virgin until I was eighteen winters old, I couldn't wait to get back home and show Oswith what I'd learned on my most recent case. My young wife was always curious about my work, and mostly it was boring stuff. If what I'd been hearing all morning was true, I didn't think she'd be bored by my souvenir evidence of the case.

As Rædnoth fiddled with the spoon he lost his grip, and it popped out of his fingers and dropped onto the table beside the body with an audible thunk. Ecgbald's wife looked up and saw what had made the noise and launched herself off the chair with a scream.

Rædnoth stumbled back, and Cenbald and Baldred intercepted their mother before she could get to the *geréfa*. She was screaming and wailing incoherently and she struck out at Rædnoth over her sons' restraining arms.

We'd been startled but soon recovered ourselves. It wasn't uncommon for grieving women to become violently transported by their sorrow, men either, for that matter. A loved one's death can make anyone temporarily insane. We'd seen it before at *gemót* courts when survivors gave testimony in murder or manslaughter cases. The two men held their mother until she calmed down and then helped her back into her chair.

What had happened wasn't all that remarkable under the circumstances, but Rædnoth and I were both interested in what had triggered her reaction. Rædnoth picked up the spoon and wound the leather thong around its handle and slipped it out of sight into his bag.

"I think we should have a word with your mother after all," I told them.

"She's upset enough," Cenbald objected.

"We won't upset her more," I promised.

"This would be a private word," Rædnoth said, looking at the door.

The older sons hesitated for a moment, realizing that we were serious. They herded their younger brothers and sisters and wives outside and closed the door after them.

Osilda sat with her eyes locked onto her husband's body.

"Why did you kill him, Osilda?" Rædnoth asked her.

"Why do you think?" she said after a moment. "All these years and he had to go with other women. Said it was because he was a man, and a man had more needs than a woman after she had seven children and dried up."

"Did you always know?"

"Not until last summer when I saw that woman in the market wearing one of the Gaulish spoons. Then I knew."

"It must have been a shock," I said.

"It was a thing for us," she said. "Not for his whores."

"How much did he tell you?"

"Said he met some women needed what he had. Said they was clean and what did I care so long as he kept them well away from me? Said it had naught to do with me."

"What happened last night?"

"I knew what he did when the forge was cold. I'm not stupid. I tried to live with it because there was nothing I could do that wouldn't cause trouble for more than him and his whores. When he didn't come home with the boys last night I got angrier and angrier because I knew what he was doing, so I waited until it was dark and I went down to the smithy to see for myself.

"I could hear them from the street—her screeching and him grunting—and I slipped into the smithy through the little door in the back and stood in the shadows and watched them. There was no fire, only a candle giving a little light. At first I couldn't move. He was having her on the work table by the forge, her on her back with her legs around him rutting into her. I looked around for a hammer to hit him with, but all the tools were across the smithy. Then I saw the rope.

"I grabbed the loose end and wrapped it around my wrist. Then I pulled the loop at the end of the pulleys out and came up behind him. He never heard me, grunting and rutting, and when I dropped the loop over his head he didn't even notice until it was too late.

"I ran back the way I'd come, and the rope went through the block and lifted him right off the ground. She had her legs wrapped around him, and she came off the table and landed on the floor, and he flew up into the air, kicking and clawing at his throat and swinging back and forth while I tied the end of the line off and stood there in the shadows and watched him swing and fight the rope.

"The woman got off the floor and all she could see was him flying through the shadows, and he kicked off his trousers and twisted around making horrible sounds, and she screamed and ran out of the smithy and didn't come back.

"When it was over I put his trousers back on him. I had to stand on the nail keg to fasten his belt and when I got down I saw how it looked, like he might have hung himself, so I knocked the keg on its side and came home."

Osilda hadn't taken her eyes off her husband's body the whole time it took her to describe his death. She would have learned all she needed to know when she was a girl on the wharf in Seletún, and then forgotten it for most of a lifetime, and then remembered it without even trying when she needed a way to pull her husband of thirty five winters off the woman he was focking, all big muscled and sweaty beside the cold forge.

This was a tricky case. If she announced the killing to Creda and took the position that she'd apprehended him in adultery she might well walk away free. I'd be willing to argue that the penalty for adultery could be legally exacted by a woman as well as a man. But what good would it do her? Her sons wouldn't understand it. I could tell from their little tutorial about the Gaulish bean spoon that their sympathies were with Ecgbald, dead over there on the table. The man who'd taught them everything they knew. And I doubted that her daughters would be more sympathetic; even if they understood the impulse, their mother had still killed their father. That's a hard one to forgive.

We couldn't just let her walk away without an explanation for the hanging because the only other explanation was suicide, and even though Ecgbald's killing was arguably justified under the laws against adultery and even though he'd flown to his death with his cock dripping the adulterous juices of a woman who was not his wife, he might have repented in those last moments. Who's to say? Maybe as the world turned black and his ears roared he experienced true remorse for his sins and was eligible for heaven, after a suitable time in purgatory to expiate his guilt. If so, he deserved to be buried in holy ground. We had to give him the benefit of the doubt.

I looked up at the rail mechanism in the rafter beams that supported the hanging cauldron and pots.

"I think you should consider entering the convent," I said to Osilda. "Many a widow has found comfort in the cloister."

Osilda looked at me as if I were speaking

Greek. I glanced at Rædnoth and saw that he was too.

"What?" I challenged him. "What good can come of dragging her in front of the *gemót* court? Her husband was committing adultery. She caught him in the act. If their positions had been reversed he would have done the same thing and everyone would understand. We're just skipping that part and getting on with the rest of life. She goes to a convent and her children never have to know she killed Ecgbald."

"So Ecgbald committed suicide?"

"Ecgbald was the unfortunate victim of a tragic accident."

I called Osilda's children back into the house and told them that I thought I knew how their father died. All of that overhead hardware had to be maintained, especially in a sooty environment like a forge or the space over a hearth in a house. Soot builds up, and pulley wheels and the runners that move cauldrons around bind and don't do their job. Suppose Ecgbald had noticed that the pulley was seizing up, and stood on the little keg to take it down so he could oil it. Suppose he shifted his weight wrong and fell and his head went into the loop and it pulled tight. Before he could even yell for help he'd be unconscious and then, well—Wibba found him the next morning.

The boys looked at one another, confused, as if they were trying that story on like an inexpensive new tunic of a questionable color to see if it fit before they handed over their coin. But before they could decide if it made sense, their mother stood up and said, "I've decided to go into a convent."

That stunned them into an even deeper bewilderment. I understood. It was a lot to take in over the course of only four or five hours: first their father was a suicide, then he was a murder victim, and then he accidentally hanged himself while performing some routine maintenance of the sort he'd done a hundred times before. Then their mother announced that she was opting for the cloistered life. The sudden loss of both parents in a single morning.

"Let's go make our report to Sentwine," I said, and Rædnoth and I expressed our condolences for their loss and left.

Sentwine was sitting at his usual table at the Barking Bitch, the Elmetsætan judiciary's favorite watering hole and source of simple, hot food in Loidis. The innkeeper was a dog lover, and he had a small pack of mutts that made themselves a nuisance under your feet but did a good job keeping the vermin in check and cleaning up anything you dropped, and they could be relied on to harry out the drunks at last call. Sentwine was still eating.

"Christ, that must have been a full Mercian breakfast," Rædnoth said.

"Breakfast was hours ago," the advocate said. "This is lunch. Where have you two been?"

"Finding out who killed the smith," I said. I gestured for Oswy, the innkeeper, to bring us a pitcher of ale and a couple of cups. When he arrived we ordered the house special—boiled sausage and mashed turnips. This was the only food they served at the Barking Bitch. Oswy liked to keep the menu simple to reduce the number of decisions his barflies had to make. He was that kind of considerate man; he'd even named all his dogs Offa to eliminate confusion.

"So did you discover the killer?" Sentwine asked.

"It was tricky," Rædnoth told him. "We had to follow clues from one end of town to the other, and we had to use our discretion in the end."

"Well, you walked a lot, and you were discrete about it. I expect no less. But did you discover the killer?"

"It was the wife," I said, pausing so he could express his amazement, but he just nodded and chewed a mouthful of mashed turnips while he cut another piece of sausage.

Rædnoth and I looked at each other.

"You act like you knew," Rædnoth said.

Sentwine swallowed his turnips and took the chunk of sausage off the point of his knife with his teeth, chewing and smiling at us.

"Why are you so surprised?" he asked. "Christ, it's always the wife."

illage Geometry

You argue that man cannot enquire either about that which he knows, or about that which he does not know; for if he knows, he has no need to enquire; and if not, he cannot; for he does not know the subject about which he is to enquire.

Meno—Socrates

Heppeworð, Elmet, 782 AD

Yesterday's rain had stopped during the night and the sky had cleared before dawn, but the drying ground was still soft under the horses' hooves. Puddles were receding in the midday sunlight. A couple of wandering goats stopped their desultory grazing and stood on their shadows to look at us and then went back to cropping weeds. There was a stone enclosure that penned in a few pigs and a smaller wattle enclosure woven of split hazel rods that was robust enough to resist a few imprisoned sheep or goats trying its resistance. There were geese and chickens, their roost boxes raised off the ground on timber frames to discourage weasels. A vegetable garden was laid out to the left of the house, surrounded by more wattle fencing to protect it from the goats.

The cunning woman uncrossed her arms and squinted up at us as we stopped the horses in front of a stone hitching post. She was wearing an undyed wool dress and a leather belt from which a pouch, sheathed knife, and scissors were suspended. She wore her hair unbound and undressed, like an unmarried virgin, and long ripples of gray framed a pointed chin and prominent cheekbones. Her tan face was crisscrossed with a net of fine wrinkles. The bridge of her nose was narrow; her eyes were sharp and almond shaped and symmetrical.

"Have you an ailment?" she asked, probably assuming that one or both of us were carrying the Gaulish pox, impervious to treatment and remorse, for which there was no cure but prayer and penance and no proof against its further spread but an abstinence that most men refused to embrace.

We dismounted, and the *geréfa* led the horses to a nearby stone trough to let them drink.

"Offa's commissioners are making a census of the hundred," I told her. "We came to ask a few questions."

"You're not a Mercian," she said.

"No. I'm the assistant advocate in the hundred *gemót*," I said. "Called Hring."

"I'm Heregyð. What do you want to ask?"

"How many people live here?"

"Only me."

"You live here alone?" The *geréfa's* brusque intrusion was characteristic. He seemed to disbelieve anything he was told. He watched us as the horses drank.

"Except for the goats and the poultry."

"What about the pigs and sheep?"

"They're meat. The goats and the fowl live here year round."

"How much land do you have?" The *geréfa's* tone seemed more antagonistic than necessary. I supposed that's why Bynna'd sent him along.

"One hide."

"That's a lot of land to work alone," I said.

"I'm in the center of a hide because that's as close as anyone wants to get to the ruins. Most of the land's gone back to the *weald*, except for the little bit I live on. People help me with the work in payment. I'm an herbalist and midwife, not a ploughman. I heal the sick, deliver babies, and set bones. Sometimes I sell stone from the villa."

I looked across the field at the ruins. "This was a big Roman estate."

"*Folc* think it's haunted."

"Is it?"

"If it is, they don't trouble me."

Heregyð smiled a carefully skeptical smile as if she were evaluating me before making some irrevocable judgment upon which she would base everything that would ever happen between us and from which she would never retreat, even in the face of contradictory evidence.

I was no stranger to irrevocable judgment, and I smiled back, unconcerned about what she decided, knowing that I'd probably never see her again, and so I was impervious to whatever judgment she might make, good or bad. All I needed from her was a minimum of cooperation and then we'd be out of one another's lives forever. Heregyð seemed about the same age as my mother's sister, and when I'd asked about her when the hidage commission was making its inquiries in Heppeworð, the village to the east, I gathered that she had a reputation for a certain unpredictable volatility. In some circles I did too, so I couldn't hold that against her; people could be volatile and have no malice in them, still I didn't want to provoke her to an uncooperative judgment, though I couldn't have said why except that I needed an hour of her time.

She had a *ceorl's* work-roughened hands, and her face and arms had been browned by the sun, and her blue eyes were a glance away from an immaculate disdain. So far she hadn't looked at the *geréfa*; her eyes were fixed on me.

"What's the tribute assessment for a single hide?"

"Depends what's on the hide. For this holding, I reckon a *thrymsa*."

The cunning woman lived alone in a house that had been one of the smaller storehouses of a Roman villa. The Romans had two kinds of country villas, the *villa urbana*, a great estate in proximity to a city that the owner could use to impress his friends and acquaintances with a weekend getaway, and the *villa rustica*, a much less grand holding given over exclusively to agricultural production, seldom visited by the master, and maintained by the servants. The cunning woman lived in the middle of what had been a *villa urbana*, close enough to Eoforwic that some rich Roman could nip down for an extended weekend of bucolic debauchery. Judging from the extent of the ruins, the owner had been quite a wealthy Roman, possibly even the provincial governor. The villa proper, a rambling complex of interconnected rooms, open atria, and enclosed gardens, something right out of Vitruvius' *De Architectura*, was now a tumbled maze of roofless walls, and here and there the floors had collapsed into the hypocaust, leaving an unstable mosaic of buckled, untrustworthy pavement. The outbuildings and slave quarters were in the same state of disintegration.

Heregyð subsisted alone on a single, underexploited hide with a small garden and a few head of livestock and what she bartered for in exchange for her wortcunning and midwifery and what she could get for reclaimed Roman stone. Still, it was a hide, and assessments are made on the size and potential of the holding, not on its actual productivity. If she could scrape up three silver pennies it would be a minor miracle of genuine interest to the pope's investigators. It was naught to me. How she paid her tribute share was between her and the *ealdorman*.

The fields that the Romans had cultivated centuries before had been reclaimed by the *weald*. We'd passed a small overgrown apple orchard that, untended, most likely produced indifferent apples that fed more wasps than people. There was a nearly evaporated pond that had once contained fish but was now a weedy marsh full of frogs and bugs. There was a big meadow watered by a meandering stream and overgrown by knee-high grasses that undulated in slow waves in a soft breeze.

A hawk floated west to east over the meadow on locked wings and grew smaller and disappeared over the tree line with the sort of effortless patience that I envied. The terrain underneath it was hilly and going anywhere on the ground in a straight line was difficult at best.

The Mercian led the horses away from the trough and tied them to the iron ring in the stone hitching post.

"Have you ever thought about the Romans who built this place?" I asked.

"I've thought about everyone who lived here; most of them were my ancestors, but you can't reckon them in the census."

I laughed. "I'm here to make certain no one does."

"I've seen you at the *gemót*."

"This summer I'm working with the hidage commission. Creda wants to be sure they don't count Roman ghosts in the tally."

She glanced at the *geréfa*. "I'm certain they wouldn't do that."

"Then you're the only one who is."

We shared a smile at the expense of all things Mercian, and Heregyð unbent a little. "Let's take a walk around the villa to set his mind at ease."

I gestured to the *geréfa* as I fell in step beside Heregyð. The *geréfa* checked the knots in the reins and followed us. The Mercian was called Eawa, and he was five or six winters older than me, half way between thirty and forty, getting long in the tooth for close work in the shield wall but rangy and more than apt to work on the hidage commission. He spoke if he was spoken to, most of the time, if he felt that speech was required, and the rest of the time he kept silent and observant and coiled to strike. He was not a man who joked or suffered jokes and he spent his days wrapped in a reserved willingness to cut your throat if you focked with him.

Eawa was decorated with the usual *gesith-man's* scars in the usual places—both forearms, his left leg, one on his left shoulder, one on his head above his left ear, and he was missing the little finger of his left hand, but his face was unmarked, which was undoubtedly why drunks and inexperienced men occasionally mistook his quietness for reluctance to fight, which mistake some of them lived to repent.

Eawa had been a *geréfa* in Bynna's commission from the beginning, handpicked from the palace guard at Tamoworthig within an hour of Bynna's appointment as a hidage commissioner. He'd served on Brorda's personal bodyguard detail and came with a good recommendation. He had sleepy killer's eyes and long hair that he wore tied at the back of his head.

Bynna had sent him along to verify my assessment of Heregyð's holding, a day trip to account for a loose end in our census of the outliers to the village of Heppeworð while the main party relocated our camp to the other side of the hundred. Bynna told me that he was sending him along to show a Mercian presence and keep me safe from wolfsheads. I accepted with thanks. I wasn't fooled by this flimsy fiction to disguise his lack of trust, and he wasn't fooled by my expressed gratitude.

Eawa caught up with us a little way down the path. A lark in the meadow sang its territorial song and another lark answered. We passed a heap of looted stone that was weedy and packed with a century of windblown dirt. Then we passed the cemetery where Heregyð's family and ancestors were buried, the graves marked by repurposed Roman stones, half of them with crosses scratched into them, some with runes. We crossed a boundary ditch on a plank bridge and then we were inside the villa proper. Heregyð led us along a low wall and through a wide space that had been a gate into the interior courtyard. There were ruins on three sides of the weedy fountain in the center, and the remains of what I reckoned had been a substantial garden wall on the fourth side.

"There's mint growing everywhere, probably has been since the Romans planted it. I've other patches of herb growing in other places." Heregyð stepped over to a thick growth and bent to pull a handful of new leaves from the plants. I could smell it as soon as she broke the stems, sharp and clean in the air. She rubbed her hands together briskly, shredding and pressing the leaves between her palms, and then dropped the crushed green pulp and covered her mouth and nose with both hands and took a deep breath.

"Love the smell," she said.

The *geréfa* began a slow circuit of the path that ran around the edge of the old garden. A row of fluted stone columns was all that remained of an arcade that had run on the three sides that fronted the main building and the two wings. More than half of them were fallen. Connected rooms opened into the arcade on one side and a wide interior hallway on the other; beyond that were the rooms on the exterior wall of the villa.

"There was a Roman villa near where I grew up," the *geréfa* said. It was only his second conversational offering in the last hour. It's a good thing I'm not one of those men who need to have all silences filled with chatter.

"How many people do you reckon lived here?" I asked.

"A family," Heregyð said. "Four or five, maybe a few more, and their slaves. I reckon this place would have supported fifty or more souls."

We followed Eawa to a semi-detached building at the end of the east range, and I saw that it had been the bath house. The three pools—*caldarium*, *tepidarium*, and *frigidarium*—were now just sunken stone cavities inside ruined walls, like three empty sockets in the jawbone of a skull; part of the *caldarium* floor had collapsed into the hypocaust below. The floors of the baths were buried in the accumulated detritus of centuries, but I knew that they were probably paved with water-themed mosaics like the remains of the Roman bath house in Eoforwic. The Romans had liked their interior decoration and their comfort, and they had skilled artisans to realize their desires. I like a nice hot bath myself, but I can't afford the mosaics.

The *geréfa* hopped down into the weedy *caldarium* and bent to look into the exposed tunnels of the hypocaust. He peered into the hole in the floor of the bath for a long moment and then stood upright. The water level would have been just at chest height. He motioned for me to join him.

"Something down here you should see."

I looked at Heregyð and then jumped down into the bath, expecting the *geréfa* to point out some animal sign. Anything could be living down there. The narrow stone passages of a hypocaust are a natural place for a badger sett or a fox den, but when I was standing beside him he pointed down into the shadows at the bottom of the hole, and I saw a woman's body, so well hidden among the brick pillars on the stone floor of the hypocaust that no one would have discovered it until the smell and the gathering ravens gave it away.

"As she's a corpse," Eawa said, "I suppose you don't want to count her."

I jumped down into the narrow space and knelt beside the body, brushing her hair back to expose her face. She was wedged against a pillar on her back, dull eyes looking up at the sky through the collapsed floor of the bath. I'd seen many a corpse, most dead of some violence, and their faces often told a story. Some seemed composed, some afraid, some surprised; the girl in the hypocaust looked betrayed, as if she'd known in her last seconds that someone she trusted had murdered her and died so quickly the realization remained on her face. I resisted the urge to stare into her glassy eyes to see the image of her murderer. There was a bunch of fresh herb in her left hand, and the front of her dress was soaked with water, although the rain had stopped hours ago; the hole was otherwise dry. Her fingers opened easily as I took the bunch of herb, and I realized that she was still warm and rigor still some way off. Her death spasm had crushed the herb in her fist.

In the confines of the narrow maze of pillars I'd smelled the astringent stink of fresh mint, and I thought at first that she'd been gathering the herb in the Roman garden, but when I looked more closely I recognized pennyroyal, an old friend from my years in the minster library, where we'd crushed dried sprigs of it into the pages of bound codices to discourage bookworm and stuffed fresh bunches of it into the pigeon holes where rolled parchment was stored. The Dog Man, my father's master of hounds, grew it near his kennels to ward off fleas. It was a versatile herb with many uses.

I put the bunch into my scrip and stood up. Several long hairs were caught in the rough masonry at about waist height and there were a few drops of blood that had run down the pillar until they dried. I reckoned that the girl had been stabbed standing at the edge of the hole in the floor of the bath and dropped immediately into the hypocaust, her head hitting the pillar, which tore out some hair and cut her scalp. I gestured for the *geréfa* to join me below floor level, and together we lifted the girl's body out of the hypocaust and lay her on the ground. There was a great pool of blood under her, and it dripped from the back of her saturated dress. I climbed out and examined her. There was a single stab wound, angled up toward her heart, just below her right shoulder blade. It had been made by a knife about two digits wide and as thick in the spine as my little finger, so I reckoned a utility knife, probably eight or ten inches long, much the same blade that hung on nearly every belt in Elmet. The only other mark was a superficial abrasion on the right side of her head where she'd scraped the bricks on the way down.

Heregyð was sitting on a fallen section of

column watching me examine the girl, wearing a stricken expression that was numb and distant. I rolled the girl onto her back and brushed her hair off her face. She seemed to be about fifteen or sixteen winters old and she had all her teeth, which were reasonably straight. She had the interchangeable good looks of young women whose faces haven't yet begun to assume their final shape. She was wearing a thick bronze bracelet incised with geometric designs on her left wrist and a pouch and knife on her woven belt. Her knife blade was clean and smelt of pennyroyal, and her pouch held a coil of string, tweezers, a spindle, and a few smooth stones. Her shoes were worn but not worn out, with sturdy leather soles, sewn with waxed linen thread, and a seam on her right shoe had been recently resewn at the instep.

I'd never seen her before, and I turned to look at Heregyð, who I'd begun to suspect was adrift in her thoughts because she'd known the dead girl well.

"What's her name?"

"Eanswiðe."

"How do you know her?"

"I'm teaching her about herbs."

"How long?"

"Four winters and a few months."

"Who might have done this?"

Heregyð shook her head slowly. "She was a good girl."

"Maybe you killed her before we got here," the *geréfa* said, matter-of-fact.

Like almost every *geréfa* of my acquaintance,

Eawa seemed eager to pin the crime on the nearest person to hand and get on with his day.

"She's still warm and limp," I said. "And her blood hasn't begun to dry. I reckon she was killed while we were talking. The killer might still be close."

The *geréfa* looked around and then drew his *seax* and started a circuit of the ruined villa, checking the rooms and then widening his search to the perimeter of the domestic property, and then beyond the ditch. The forest encroached within twenty yards of the ruins on the north side, and there didn't seem any profit to be had from trying to pick up the killer's trail in the trees.

While the Mercian was looking for sign, I regretted the absence of even the poorest tracker in Sentwine's *hird* (Eggard), so deficient in the craft that he could only distinguish one set of wolf prints from another, while the best tracker (Anláf) could tell you what both wolves had eaten for lunch.

"Did you know she was here?"

Heregyð shook her head. Her reaction was strong and genuine. She wiped her eyes with the backs of her wrists.

"She was here yesterday asking about the uses of an herb. She said she might come back today."

"Who'd want to kill her?"

"No one that I know."

"Where did she live?"

"In Heppeworð. Her father's the village *geréfa*."

I remembered the father from the hidage commission's visit to Heppeworð. The local *thegn* had sent his tally of the village and his *tún* to the *ealdorman*, and we'd gone to verify his numbers. Because the tally only included the heads of families, it was down to us to flesh out the true population figures, and we'd dealt with the two tithing men, the village *geréfa*, and *tún-geréfa*. The *thegn* was off hunting and couldn't be bothered.

"They have to be told," I said. "Did you know her family well?"

She nodded, her eyes on the dead girl.

"Then come with me while I do it."

When Eawa returned from his scout to the edge of the woods he helped me carry the girl's body to Heregyð's house and lay her on the long work table near the hearth. The bloody dress had blotted up dirt and grass from the ground when I examined the body, and it was a red, muddy business.

The interior of the building was a single room, longer than wide; the third that was fenced off for the wintering of livestock showed no recent evidence that livestock had been stabled there. A second third of the room was Heregyð's living space, and the remaining third was her work space. The work area was marked by hanging bunches of dried herbs, crucibles, mortars and pestles, retorts, a separate small hearth and a small clay oven—all the mechanisms and apparatus for reducing herbs to their essential oils, concocting and decocting remedies, making charms, salves and poultices, and conducting the routine business of a cunning person.

In a society of little mobility, most people are content to remain immobile and make the best of their place in the world, however limited their opportunities or constricted their options, even if they resent their place in life. But some people long for more, even in the little world they know, and resist the anesthetic immobility of resentment. They use their resentment to fuel their search for something more, and looking at the body of the daughter of the *geréfa* of a little village, I suspected I was looking at someone who'd longed for more scope than birth and class had made available and tried to do something about it.

There are all sorts of mobility in the world, locomotion not the most satisfying and sometimes the least. I knew that the mobility of the mind, the transportation of knowledge, was sometimes the best and sometimes the worst, and I reckoned that the girl's attempt to better her station by learning wortcunning was the most attractive available to her, and one that would incidentally benefit her village.

"How far are we from Heppeworð?"

"A little over a mile," she said.

I looked at the *geréfa*. "I guess we're going back to the village."

Heregyrð collected her cloak and water flask and slung a sack over her shoulder, as voluminous as a saddle bag and packed with the supplies of her occupation, and met us at the hitching post. She stepped up on a stone block that was set on the ground for the purpose and swung her leg over the horse's rump and put her hands on my waist. Instead of retracing our way to the road she directed us across the meadow, where the ground was soft and yielding, through the shallow stream, and then into the trees to the east on a trail that traffic to and from the village had improved into a wide path. We rode single file, the Mercian behind.

I regretted again the absence of even the least accomplished tracker in Sentwine's *hird*, who might have been able to read the story written in the dirt of the path—who had come or gone, how long ago they'd passed—skills I'd never learned growing up in the minster, wasting my time instead on Latin and Greek, and the disciplines of the Trivium and Quadrivium.

"She was clutching a bunch of pennyroyal when I found her," I said.

"Where did you learn to recognize herbs?"

"At the minster in Eoforwic."

"A curious study for an advocate."

"At the time I thought I was studying to become a *mæsse-thegn*."

"A *mæsse-thegn*," she repeated, her tone communicating a certain disappointment in her experience of *mæsse-thegns*—a judgment that was already rendered and not up for review.

"They threw me out in my eighteenth winter."

We rode for another hundred yards without talking.

"I don't suppose that she had a library to safeguard from bookworm," I said. "Or a dog troubled by fleas?"

The cunning woman was silent.

"Upset stomach, then? Odiferous farts? A persistent cold? I knew a woman in Eoforwic who kept a pleasure house much frequented by the *thegns* of the more wealthy kindreds," I said. "She had another use for pennyroyal, when carelessness or accident required it."

Heregyð realized that I was learned enough in wortcunning to understand the basic uses of pennyroyal, however I'd come by the knowledge, and I reckoned she knew I had a good idea what the intended use of the penny-royal had been and that confidentiality about the girl's visit was a waste of time—all that was left was to limit her complicity as much as she could.

"That use is a sin before God and a crime before the king," Heregyð said.

"Knowledge is knowledge," I shrugged. "The use of knowledge may be against the law or not, or sinful or not, but merely knowing a thing isn't a crime. As far as I know the girl had a problem with fleas. In any case, you were talk-ing to us, not preparing herbs that would make a pregnant girl abort."

"Are you certain she had pennyroyal? It looks a lot like mint."

I took some of the herb from my scrip and held it to the side so she could inspect it; then I crushed it in my fist.

"It smells a bit like spearmint, but stronger, and the leaves are smoother and not so veined." I turned my hand and let the bruised herb fall to the ground. "It's supposed to weave peace between husband and wife, and it wards off evil if you mix it with nettle and graveyard dirt."

We rode through a birch grove, the serrated leaves quivering in the sunlight. "Eanswiðe was in love with someone in the village," she said after a little while. "She never told me his name, as much as she talked about his virtues— handsome, strong, brave, and smart—all the lies an inexperienced girl in love tells herself."

Heregyð's familiarity with the lies an experienced girl tells herself made me wonder about her own experience as an inexperienced girl, but I let it pass.

"Was she going to marry this ideal young man?"

"No."

"Why not?"

"One of the usual reasons I reckon—he was a *thegn*, or already married, or didn't love her back, or one of the families disapproved."

I silently listed a few more reasons from my experience in the *gemót* court, where many a father had appealed many a man for despoiling his virgin daughter, and the appealed man always looked affronted by the accusation and, with his cock safely tucked away, denied his guilt.

"There's another man who loves Eanswiðe," Heregyð said. "But she had her heart set on the one she couldn't have."

How often is that the story in life? How often does it end badly? Although not always with a knife in the back and a body dumped in a Roman ruin.

We rode out of the woods into the plough land that surrounded Heppeworð. Some of the ground was unbroken and fallow; other strips had been planted in barley and rye and were in good growth. A ploughman and his two sons were preparing for the second planting, turning over dark furlongs in the rain-softened earth behind a full team of eight oxen; the younger boy walked behind the team breaking up the clods; the older boy kept the oxen moving with the long goad while their father guided the plough. The field was half finished and the oxen were well into the second acre of long furrows. When they saw us the older son and the father kept the plough moving but the young boy breaking the clods succumbed to curiosity and stood still to watch us while the team pulled away from him until his father whistled him back to work.

The village of Heppeworð was a long, curved, climbing street on a bench of land half way up the hill. There were houses on either side of the street and communal barns and stables in the center where the ox teams were kept and for the village farming activities. The villagers were busy with the industry of the month: shepherds were castrating lambs and docking their tails, village boys were weeding tares from the furlongs of rye and barley, women were weaving. The village dogs barked at us, and before we were half way up the hill a few men had gathered to meet us. I could smell bread baking.

Most villages are only composed of a few families surrounded by their fields or their woods. Most villages are separated from one another by at least a mile or two. Many steadings are the property of a single family. The usual distribution of people in the southern hundreds of Elmet made it hard for the hidage commission to efficiently gather information, necessitating a number of trips to verify the numbers that the *thegn*s provided to the commissioner.

Heppeworð was unusual because it was by comparison a large village with the population and its appurtenances and livestock collected in a single location with only a few outliers. There were two tithings in Heppeworð—twenty three families—a total of seventy-three men women and children together with another thirty-six more in the *tún*. There was a church. There was a mill on the river at the base of the hill and a couple of weirs. At the top of the hill there had been a *ráth*, a Celtic hill fort, but when Elmet had fallen to Northumbria the local Celts had relocated west to live among the Wealsch tribes and a Northumbrian *thegn* had settled on the high ground, dismantled or repurposed the circular houses, improved the earthwork and ditch, and used the stone the Celts had looted from the Roman ruin to make a wall to surround his timber hall and the houses of his *ceorls*. In the time of the Celts the top of the hill had apparently been covered in larch trees, their shady, feathery branches swaying gracefully in every passing wind, but those trees had been cut long ago and were now commemorated only by the name *Larchtún*.

The *tún geréfa* had authority over the village, but there was also a village *geréfa* and two tithing men to take care of the daily operations and keep order. They must not have much to do in their capacity as civic administrators because the villagers of Heppeworð were law abiding *ceorls*—I didn't remember anyone from Heppeworð ever being appealed before the *gemót* for so much as harsh language in a fit of temper. Perhaps they weren't especially litigious, preferring to settle their disputes among themselves.

We stopped our horses where the road leveled out and became the main street. The men waiting there showed no signs of giving ground until they knew the matter of our business. Heregyð slipped off the horse and started into the village without bothering to make any introductions and the men gave her a familiar nod as she passed them.

"We've business with the village *geréfa*," I said.

"We thought we'd seen the last of you," one of the men said.

"You're the advocate with the Mercians, aren't you?" the other one asked.

"Assistant advocate," I corrected him. "Name's Hring."

"Better get off your horses, then. Get neck ache looking up at you."

We dismounted and led the horses up the village street to the big stable. The men who'd waited for us walked along.

"Is the priest here?"

"You're in luck if you want a confession; today's his day to listen to sins."

"We'll need him, I think. Can you tell him we're here?"

One of the men walked away toward the church.

"Where's the village *geréfa*? I can't remember his name."

"Æsc. He's ploughing his furlongs."

The hill the village and *tún* occupied was surrounded by plough land, and as I hadn't recognized the man I'd seen gouging furrows, I reckoned Æsc was working his team on the other side of the hill. Eawa took the reins from my hand and led both horses along the fence that enclosed the stable yard and into the stable, where he began to unsaddle them. He seemed to think this was going to take some time. There was still a team of oxen inside the stable yard, eight bovine hulks standing motionless except for their swishing tails, keeping their eyes on the activity. One of them yawned and licked its nose. Another one released a load of shite onto the ground, to the delight of the flies.

Heregyð was returning with another woman who I assumed must be the dead girl's mother. She didn't seem distraught, so I knew the cunning woman had reserved the job of announcing her daughter's death for me. After half a summer of telling people how much tribute they owed the Mercians I was getting used to the conscientious discharge of unpleasant responsibility.

Delivering news of a death is a little like killing the person yourself. Whoever you tell will always associate the knowledge of that death with you, and if the death is significant to them, how they think of the dead person will ever after be divided into the time before you told them and the time after, and your face will be the fulcrum that holds those times in balance. I'd spoken the death words to enough people that I didn't want to do it in the street, where the girl's mother would be exposed to that moment of raw public grief.

I glanced at Eawa, who was setting one of the saddles on the stall rail, and started forward to intercept Heregyð and Eanswiðe's mother. I met the two women not far from the church and steered them in that direction as I introduced myself to the dead girl's mother.

"This is Leola," Heregyð said, starting to drop back, but I could see from the way the two women acted that they were easy with one another and I jerked my head toward the church to indicate I wanted Heregyð to come inside with us. It would be better for the mother if she was with someone she knew when I told her that her daughter was dead. The man who'd gone to fetch the priest stepped out of the church door.

"Priest's busy."

"We'll wait."

The church was a medium size building that would be filled to capacity if the whole village came to mass, a good thing in the winter cold but uncomfortably close in the summer heat. The interior was shaded and noticeably cooler out of the sun. The plank floor wasn't quite level and it undulated from front to back in a pattern of uneven settling. The altar was a wooden table that was covered with a fine embroidered linen altar cloth. The priest was sitting on a bench in the sanctuary, his head bent forward in prayer, and a young man was sitting on the bench with him, also praying. I saw that we'd interrupted him at confession and waited inside the door.

Heregyð looked at the priest and puckered her lips as if she'd just bitten into a mealy, sour apple from her untended orchard, and I sighed and braced for more trouble still. It looked to me as if the not unusual animosity of priests and cunning persons existed between these two, often the case when a cunning person's success rate, which depends on the logical diagnosis and treatment of earthly maladies, exceeds the priest's, which depends on prayer and luck to mitigate spiritual ills. Occasionally a priest and a cunning person manage to work together for the benefit of a village, but more often the priest takes himself too seriously or the cunning person doesn't take the priest seriously enough, or there might be some past friction between the two, or some other sort of jealousy, any of which might end in accusations of witchcraft if the cunning person wasn't careful.

When we came into the church the priest and the man he was confessing looked up at us and the man lowered his voice and turned his face away. The priest whispered to him and put a hand on his shoulder briefly, imparting the touch of forgiveness and acceptance that might sooth the confessional guilt.

The priest refused to be rushed through the sacrament, and I could see Eanswiðe's mother getting anxious, having correctly concluded that the presence of an assistant advocate and Heregyð, her daughter's teacher in wort-cunning, with news that they wanted to deliver in the church, meant nothing good.

The sound of voices outside, loud and getting louder, meant that I'd waited long enough for the priest. Heregyð looked out the door and turned to Leola. "Your husband's coming."

The village geréfa walked into the church and hesitated to accustom his eyes to the dim light. When his eyes adjusted he located his wife and went to stand with her. He smelled like a man who'd been sweating his way through the shite behind an ox team for the better part of the day, and I could see that the patience that occupation demanded was fast falling away, replaced by anxious movement from side to side as he shifted his weight on his feet.

"Are you Eanswiðe's mother and father?"

"What's happened to her?"

"Someone killed her," I said. There was no

use wasting time attempting to prepare them—best out with it and get on to the unpleasantness of their reaction. Leola covered her open mouth with a hand, as if she were stifling a silent wail; Æsc wrung his hands and took a step backward. The death of hope is always a terrible thing to see, and the death of a parent's hope for a child is the worst.

"Where? When?"

"At the Roman ruin. Less than an hour ago."

"Where is she?"

"My house," Heregyð said.

Just then a man ran up to the church door and skidded inside. He was younger than Eanswiðe's father, closer to the dead girl's age, and messier. There was blood on his trousers and tunic and the backs of both hands.

"What's the matter? Has something happened to Eanswiðe?"

Eanswiðe's mother wiped the tears off her cheeks and took his hands. "She's dead."

The man endured a few seconds of stunned disbelief, looking from face to face, and I watched hopes and plans for his future crumble behind his eyes. The man looked at Eanswiðe's father, who nodded, verifying what didn't need verification, and he took a slow deep shuddering breath, stunned by the blunt, instrumental knowledge of Eanswiðe's death.

I remembered Heregyð's concise account of the girl's private life and reckoned this was the man who loved her while she loved someone else. I understood that lingering ache and the relief to be had from denial and hope, which

Eanswiðe's mother had taken away with two words. Eanswiðe wouldn't be coming to her senses now with the realization of who really loved her best; there would be no recovering from rejection in the comfort of his patient presence. All possibility of that was gone.

"She's waiting for us at Heregyð's house," Eanswiðe's father said to him. "Will you help me bring her home, Ósmód?"

The man, identified as Ósmód, nodded and they walked unsteadily out of the church together into the sunlight. Heregyð put her arms around Leola and held her as she wept silently for her daughter.

Heregyð was facing the altar and she looked beyond me and her mouth twitched as if she were suppressing an impulse to spit out that sour thing she'd tasted earlier. I turned around and saw that the priest was walking down the length of the church. The man he'd confessed was still on the bench in the sanctuary.

As he got closer I remembered that the *mæsse-thegn* wasn't what I'd expected when I met him the week before. He wasn't a pinch-faced, skinny aesthetic exiled to a small village and steeped in the frustration of listening to the same sins committed by the same people and absolving them with the same token penances so they could go forth and commit them again with clear consciences. Neither did he seem to be mired in the complacency of a village priest who was happy with a comfortable and unde-manding life in a place that prospered enough in its small way that everyone survived the dim, cold months between Christmas and Easter.

The reality was much worse: he was eager to help us accomplish our task, friendly and pleasant to work with. He was smooth faced, ruddy, hale, and well-fed, and he was the sort of priest who took his mission seriously, even though it was in the dull, agricultural southern hundreds of Elmet and not the exciting, tangled forests of Germania, where the Saxons still worshipped the grim old forest gods of their fathers with blood sacrifices and not the son of the grim old desert God of the Hebrews with bloodless, symbolic ritual and tithes. Of all the sorts of priests I'd encountered in the minster of Eoforwic, I most disliked the zealous true believers, especially when they were unsupervised in their belief.

The *mæsse-thegn*, fresh from hearing confession, retained that glow that priests sometimes acquire when they've been acting as a conduit for human repentance and divine forgiveness— an aura of drifty sanctity that was the residue of their communion with God. Like the warmth your clothing absorbs when standing close to a fire in the winter, I knew it wouldn't last long.

I could feel the tension rolling off Heregyð like heat waves radiating off stony ground. She eased away from Leola, into the shadows beside the open door of the church, until her back touched the whitewashed wall.

"I'm Benedict," the priest said.

"Hring, assistant to the advocate Sentwine in the hundred *gemót*."

"I remember you. Why have you come back

so soon?"

The *mæsse-thegn* was one of those priests who'd shed his old name like a snakeskin and assumed the name of a person he admired, in this case the creator of the Rule that governed organized monastic life. It was an affectation that was just coming into vogue about the time I'd been expelled from the minster in Eoforwic, and now, ten winters later, it seemed finally to be seeping into the hinterland of the rural hundreds.

"The girl Eanswiðe has been murdered," I said.

The priest stepped toward Leola and put his left hand on her head and traced a cross in the air with his right as he murmured a Latin blessing. His pronunciation was perfect, advertising his training at one of the more rigorous monastic schools, in the south, to judge by his accent.

"I see you've already apprehended the one responsible." He looked at Heregyð standing with her back to the wall and then at me.

"Why do you think so?"

"Eanswiðe was learning the ways of the devil, and the devil will have his due."

I was disappointed. Resorting to enigmatic aphorisms ought to be beneath someone who pronounced his Latin as beautifully as this man did.

"What's that supposed to mean?"

Challenged, the *mæsse-thegn* hesitated, and then he said, "Heregyð uses the methods of Satan to entice the weak and afflicted, and she was teaching her witchcraft to Eanswiðe. I told the girl to renounce this knowledge, and when she did, it's plain Heregyð must have stabbed her."

"Do you have proof of this accusation? Do you want to appeal her for murder?"

"When you have true knowledge of a thing, proof is unnecessary."

"Really? Then all those hours my Rhetoric tutor at the minster school in Eoforwic spent stressing the need to support an argument with factual proof were a waste of time. He seemed to think that inspired knowledge without proof is nothing but ignorance passing as truth."

I could see the lingering bliss from his confessional communion with God melt away.

"Although," I continued. "It's curious you knew she was stabbed when I only said she'd been murdered."

The *mæsse-thegn* opened his mouth and closed it again, thinking the better of whatever he'd intended to say.

"Inspiration?" I prompted.

The man on the bench in the sanctuary stood and crossed himself, his penance apparently accomplished, and walked around the altar and into the nave, toward the door. He was wearing better thread than anyone I'd seen in the village so far, clothing that hadn't been woven for field work, clothing that most *ceorls* would keep in a cedar chest for wearing once a year at Easter mass. As he got closer I realized that his clothes only made sense if he was a son of the village *thegn*. He was sporting a fine brown tunic with embroidery at the hems and a tooled belt with silver studs that held a sheath, a bag, and a water bottle, all fashioned from dyed leather and all three recently stained dark by the moisture of a spilled liquid. On the skin of his left wrist there was an established green stain. The man tried to slip past us, eyes downcast, still concentrating on the remission of his sins. I stepped to my left and blocked his progress.

"Who are you?" I asked.

The man looked at me and saw that bluster would avail him nothing. He glanced at the *mæsse-thegn*.

"Don't you know?" I asked him. "Do you need the *mæsse-thegn* to consult his vast store of unproven knowledge and supply the answer?"

"I'm called Ansgar," he said.

"How hard was that? Did you know Eanswiðe?"

He hesitated, and I could see that he wanted to look at the *mæsse-thegn* again but controlled himself and looked at the floor instead.

"Is the answer down there between your feet?"

"I knew her."

"Are you surprised to hear that she's dead?"

Ansgar looked grieved but not altogether shocked at the news. He stammered a moment before he managed to croak, "Dead?" I looked at the confessionally sealed *mæsse-thegn*, whose face betrayed nothing.

"How long have you been hearing confessions?"

"Since I was ordained." The priest smiled a disingenuous, smart-arsed smile.

"How long today?"

"Ansgar was the first to seek absolution to-day."

"What were you doing before that?"

"My pastoral duties about the church."

I nodded and turned to Heregyð, who was once again comforting the crying woman. "Let's go."

The Mercian *geréfa* Eawa had finished stabling the horses and was walking around Heppeworð asking questions and being given contradictory and unhelpful answers. Word of the girl's death hadn't circulated yet, and the villagers assumed we'd returned to clear up a few misunderstandings with the hidage count and they were having their fun with him, not yet grasping that absent cooperation he was free to invent his own figures, which could only be the worse for them when the *ealdorman* came to collect the tribute. In the meanwhile they were taking the piss out of him with a rustic vacuity that allowed them to safely enjoy withholding information. He saw me and Heregyð and the dead girl's mother walk out of the church and came over to join us.

The village was small, and it was a short walk to Leola's house, where everything was sure to remind her of her daughter. When we were inside Heregyð stoked the fire in the hearth and put a pot of water on to boil. She opened her bag and sorted through the supplies she'd brought, taking out two soft goatskin bags from which she shook what looked like the dried leaves of lemon balm and valerian root into a cup—both with restorative properties that would calm the emotions.

When the water boiled she poured it into the cup and the hot liquid released a pleasant smelling steam. She gave it to Leola, who held it in both hands, blowing on the surface and breathing the steam until it was cool enough to drink.

I opened the door and motioned to Heregyð to follow me outside. She joined me a moment later. Eawa waited on a bench in the shade, frowning at the general drift of his day so far. "Word's starting to spread," he said.

"What's the matter between you and the *mæsse-thegn*?" I asked Heregyð.

"A year ago a flux came to the village. He preached that it was a punishment for sin and forbade the *folc* to ask me for treatment. Said it was a penance they had to accept. Most of the *folc* listened, but a few families asked me for help. All of them got better in a few days. The ones that listened to him and fasted and prayed for forgiveness were sick for a week and five of them died—three children and an old man and a pregnant woman. Since then, sick *folc* come to me before they go to him, and he says I've lured them away from God with the devil's wiles."

"Haven't you lived here all your life?"

"I have, but he only came two years ago when the old priest died."

"How long was the old priest here?"

"Since I was a child."

I glanced in the direction of the church.

Ansgar walked out the door and hesitated, looking around the street, and when he saw us standing at the threshold of Leola's house he walked away. The *mæsse-thegn* stood just inside the door, in the interior shadows of the church. I couldn't see his face, but I could feel the weight of his gaze.

"Did Eanswi∂e always wear that bronze bracelet?"

"I never saw it before."

Heregy∂ went back into the house to check on Leola, and I joined Eawa on the bench and caught him up on the happenings inside the church.

"I reckon you have to get involved in this," he said.

I nodded. "This village is in my advocate's jurisdiction. Someone will be appealed for the girl's killing at the next *gemót*, and he'll want to know as much as possible. He always prefers it when whoever's appealed for a crime is the one who actually did it."

An expression of faint amazement flickered across Eawa's face at hearing this strange idea, but he said nothing. The villagers were going about their work almost as if we weren't there, but I knew that their routine had been altered and affected by the murder in ways that we, unfamiliar with the quotidian rhythms of their lives, couldn't recognize. I looked down the street toward the church. No one else seemed inclined to confess today.

"If you want to go back to the *hird* I'll see this through without you."

"Nothing but more work waiting there," Ea-wa said. "I'll stick in case you need me."

"Any ideas about what might have happened to the girl?"

"I think you're right the cunning woman had nothing to do with it. Maybe it was the priest. You said he didn't like the girl learning about herbs and he dislikes the cunning woman. He could've gone to the ruins and killed the girl so he could blame it on her, get rid of the two of them at once."

I considered his theory for a minute.

"It should be easy enough to find out if he left the village this morning. The quickest route would take him past those ploughmen at the bottom of the hill, and he'd have to take the quickest way to get back ahead of us."

"The man with blood all over him seemed interested in what happened."

"He loved the dead girl."

"Like that's never been a reason to kill someone."

"Lots of farm work makes you bloody," I said. "But we can find out about him as well. The boy the priest was confessing knew the girl, and he was upset about something."

"Come to that, in a place this size everyone knew the girl. Maybe they'll be more helpful to you than they were to me."

Heregyð came back with a basket of dried apples and a jug of water and a couple of links of sausage and went back inside while we ate. The sky remained clear and the breeze dropped off and I thought how considerate of the killer to give me good weather for the investigation. I closed my eyes and said a prayer for guidance. Eawa leaned against the wall and relaxed. Women began to arrive as the news of Eanswiðe's death moved through the village. Soon the house was full of women offering comfort to Leola, diminishing her grief not in the slightest but maybe showing her that she wasn't quite so alone.

Heregyð finally sent them packing with thanks for their concern and assurances that they'd made it possible for Leola to survive the worst a mother had to endure. It's strange how moving even a small and offhand kindness can be when it's sincerely offered. Oswith once told me that when I talked about the minster she could tell how hard it had been to come back to my kindred after ten winters preparing for a life and a future that had been stolen from me. It was then that I began to love her, because I don't think there can be love without understanding, and she was the only one who seemed to understand.

As the women dispersed to their homes, two men walked down the sloping street from the direction of the hilltop *tún*. I nudged the Mercian with my elbow and he opened his eyes.

"Unless I'm much mistaken, this is the village *thegn* and his *tún geréfa*."

"I remember the *geréfa*," Eawa agreed. "Never saw the *thegn*."

Geometry, my instructor at the minster used to say, is concerned with the relationships of objects in space. It emerged from Euclid's mind as a set of self-evident axioms to become a majestic system of deductive propositions. Geometry is logic, and logic is geometric in its perfection. I smoothed the dirt with my foot and began to draw figures in the dust with the point of my *seax*, remembering the *Meno* as I worked, and smiling at how Plato's students must have reacted when he described that old fox Socrates demonstrating that the slave was an unknowing geometer all along.

I drew squares that might have represented the houses in the village on either side of a line that might have represented the street and a polygon that might have represented the walled *tún* at the top of the hill and a scattering of small rectangles a distance from the rest that possibly represented the Roman ruins and Heregyð's house, as a hawk might see them looking down as it drifted on the thermals the way that hawk had earlier in the day.

Then I described arcs between some of the buildings and joined others with straight lines, extending some, connecting others, drawing a triangle with the points at the church, the *tún*, and Heregyð's steading. Everything in life is Geometry, because what are we if not objects in relationship to one another?

A static Geometry may be calculated with patience and logic, so the Geometry of a settled society where everyone's fixed in their roles and expectations and content with their hierarchical position may be easily solved and will yield reliably predictable and reproducible results. The Geometry of a dynamic society is more difficult to calculate; constantly changing relationships have constantly changing solutions, dynamic chaos is unknowable and unpredictable and scares the shite out of anyone who gives it much thought, and when murder disturbs the social Geometry, what have you got but a steaming plate of chaos?

Eawa cleared his throat and I looked up to see the *thegn* and the *geréfa* standing a few paces away watching me.

"Are you the advocate?" the *thegn* asked.

"Assistant advocate, called Hring," I nodded.

"You questioned my son about the girl who was killed?"

"I only asked him if he knew her."

"Of course he knew her. Everyone knows everyone here."

"He was confessing when I went into the church to find the priest."

"He's devout." The *thegn* was twisting his neck in an attempt to decipher the drawings I'd made in the dirt, and I erased them with my foot.

"Is he indeed?"

"What do you intend to do?"

I stood up and gestured at Ósmód and Æsc, back from the Roman ruins, who were pulling a cart containing Eanswiðe's body toward the house.

"I'm going to let these people see to their daughter and while they do I'm going to talk to *folc* in the village. When we finish here, we'll be up to talk to you and your son." I slipped my *seax* back into the scabbard.

The *mæsse-thegn* came out of the church and walked to meet the two men pulling the cart. He walked beside them, but I noticed that he didn't offer to replace either of them at the cart shaft. Heregyð came out of the house and walked to the other side of the street as they pulled the cart to the door of the house. Ósmód and Æsc lifted Eanswiðe's body out of the cart and carried her inside. They looked exhausted by the effort of pulling the cart and I knew why: a cartload of memories and ruined expectations and disappointment is a lot heavier than a mere nine stone of dead weight, and it had sapped their strength to pull it all the way from the Roman ruins. There was a wail from Eanswiðe's mother when she saw her daughter. The priest looked at me and Eawa and followed them inside. The *thegn* and the *tún-geréfa* walked away, and I motioned Heregyð back.

"Let's spend this little while talking to the *folc*," I said.

We started a circuit of the village. The reluctance to talk created by the presence of the Mercian was balanced by the tongue-loosening effect of Heregyð's presence, known and apparently liked by everyone but Benedict the *mæsse-thegn*, and the villagers were forthcoming in their answers.

"Ósmód loved her since they was ankle bit-ers," the blacksmith said as he pounded the end of an iron rod into the shape of a spoon bowl. The forge was in the center of the village, and you could see most of what went on in either direction on the street, so I thought it was a good place to start.

"See that coal? It's all about the temperature of the iron. Too hot and the iron burns and it's brittle when it cools. Too cool it won't get soft enough to work. That's the color of the coals you want when you're working bog iron," he said. "Different color than you need when you're working a blade. You want bluer then."

"Ósmód might have loved her," the woman at the loom said as she tossed the shuttle through the spread threads of the warp. "But to Eanswiðe he was a brother, more like." She packed the weave with the wooden shed stick and opened the warp again. "In pagan days they thought your *wyrd* was woven on the loom."

At the dairy barn we watched a cat dance on its hind legs while a milk maid squirted it in the face with a stream of warm milk straight from the teat. "Eanswiðe set her cap for Ansgar this winter," the milk maid said. "By spring it looked like she had him. He's third son of the *thegn* Ælfnóth, and his kindred have lived on the *tún* since the Celts left." She glanced around to see if anyone was close enough to overhear us. "You never heard it from me, but Ansgar's a twitchy little shite who thinks the sun don't set on his fair good looks."

"You can tell when a man's getting it regular," the thresher said as he wound cord around the long handle of a flail, sitting beside the threshing floor, "and that turd Ansgar was getting it until the midsummer feast. They had a focking row like two cats in a sack, and then he wasn't getting it no more." That was all he had to say on the subject, and he tied the new hemp grip on the flail handle and stood and took a few diagnostic whacks, raising dust from the threshing floor, and then satisfied with the work, walked away.

At the shearing barn where Ósmód worked his friends were at first reluctant to disclose anything they thought might embarrass him, but after a little coaxing they opened up. "Ósmód was with us all day nutting lambs and clipping their tails." The shepherd indicated a pile of tails and a bucket of meaty, egg-shaped lumps, all bloody and attracting flies. There was blood all over him and the other two who were dragging in the bleating lambs and then laughing as, absent tails and balls, they wobbled off in mutilated surprise.

"Just after the midsummer feast—" one of them started to say, and got a kick in the ankle for his trouble.

"We heard that Ansgar and Eanswiðe had a fight at the festival," the cunning woman said.

"That fight was nothing," the shepherd said, rubbing an ankle and glaring at his mate who'd kicked him. "T'was the one after the festival I'm talking about. Happened right here."

His friend the kicker said, "You'd think all

these balls would go to waste, but my ma has a recipe makes 'em melt in your mouth." Then he started into the details of his mother's recipe for cooking lambs balls, and we couldn't get them back to the details of the fight.

Those details had skittered to the wood turner's shed across the street from the shearing barn while we learned all about the culinary stylings of the shepherd's mother, and we had to catch up with them there.

"We heard about the fight Ansgar and Eanswiðe had at the midsummer festival, but what about the one she had with Ósmód at the shearing barn?"

The wood turner looked up from the spinning axis of the pole lathe. "Ósmód never had no fight with Eanswiðe; that was Ansgar."

"Ansgar? What were they fighting about?"

"Couldn't tell you," the wood turner said. "From here it was all just mumbles, but I could see right enough they was hot as badgers with sticks up their arses. Didn't last long but next thing you know Ósmód punched Ansgar right in the middle of his pasty face and put him on his arse." He frowned and looked at the bowl he was turning on the lathe. "My old da used to make two nested bowls out of the same block right on the lathe," he said. "But the grain has to cooperate and you have to do it by feel alone. Can't look into the space between the bowls. Was a thing to see."

The potter was working at the stone kiln just beside the wood turner. He was grubby with clay and charcoal from making up the fire and bitching like an old grandmother. "I saw Eanswiðe leave the village early this morning," he said. "I reckoned she was going to your place." He nodded at the cunning woman. "I can't talk now, though, I got to tend the kiln. You don't pay attention to the firing for even a minute you can ruin a whole run of pots and waste a day and a night."

The thatcher was splitting hazel rods to weave into wattle panels, and although he didn't stop working he spared enough of his attention to talk to us. "Ansgar's been spending time with the priest lately. I reckon he's thinking of taking up the religious life. Not much for a third son to inherit."

"Did he say he's going to profess, or are you just guessing?"

"Said naught," the thatcher shrugged. "Stands to reason, though, don't it? Never saw him with the priest before, now they're thick as thieves. Just this early morning him and the *mæsse-thegn* was talking and then he left and the *mæsse-thegn* was out in front of the church pulling weeds in the foundation until Ansgar got back."

A number of other villagers with occupations that gave them an unrestricted view of some section of the village street told us enough for us to understand that Ansgar had run up the hill, up the street, and into the church not long before we came to Heppeworð.

When we finished our circuit of the village we had added to our general fund of knowledge in a number of areas (except the threshing of grain), and it was clear to me that the Geometry of the triangle that existed with Ósmód, Eanswiðe, and Ansgar at its three points was scalene and unbalanced, but I thought that if I applied myself with diligence I could find the answer I needed.

We presented ourselves at Eanswiðe's house a couple of hours later. There was a milling crowd of mourners inside and out, speaking in low respectful voices of the dead girl and louder angry voices about the violation of their *mund* and the killing of someone they all knew and liked. Eanswiðe was lying on the sleeping platform, washed and dressed for eternal sleep, and her mother and father sat at her head and feet. Someone had collected flowers and arranged them around the body, and the blossoms had combined with the mint trod underfoot in the rushes to release a sweet scent that was immediately noticeable when you walked into the house. Neighbor women had brought refreshments and some of the men had brought a funeral libation of mead to lubricate their grief.

I slipped through the crowd and located Ósmód, who was standing against the wall with his eyes fixed on Eanswiðe. In his distraction he hadn't thought to clean himself up, and the blood had dried on his tunic and hands a dark reddish brown. The *mæsse-thegn* Benedict was praying over the body. There was a glisten of oil on her forehead and lips, an indication that the priest had administered the last rites, giving her the benefit of the contritional doubt.

"Ósmód," I said. "I'm going to the *tún* and I'd like you to come with me."

"Why?"

"Because I think you can help with my inquiry."

He looked back at Eanswiðe, reluctant to leave her now, and I noticed that the *mæsse-thegn* had abandoned his prayers and was walking toward us.

"What are you doing here?"

"Finishing my inquiry," I said. "I've only to walk up to the *tún* and I'll have everything I need."

"The *tún*? Why?"

"I've some questions to ask."

"Haven't you disturbed these people enough?"

"Not quite. There's a little more disturbance to come."

I took Ósmód's arm and turned away, but the priest followed us out of the house. Eawa and Heregyð were waiting, and when she and the priest saw one another there was a frisson of ill will inappropriate to the mournful tone of the occasion, but how often have funeral rites been the venue for the untimely eruption of suppressed feelings? Twenty or twenty-five percent of the time in my experience, and under these circumstances I'd have been surprised if they hadn't. I started up the street toward the *tún* and Heregyð, the *mæsse-thegn*, and Ósmód followed; Eawa brought up the rear so he could keep an eye on everyone.

We climbed the hill without conversation to slow us down, and presented ourselves at the gate of the *tún* where a gatekeeper, who'd seen us coming, waited to admit us. The *tún* had a great defensive situation on the hilltop, commanding all approaches, and the stone wall, while not much of a flatland fortification, combined with original Celtic ditch and berm and the slope of the hill to give defenders a significant tactical advantage. The entire village population could shelter there if necessary.

"We're here to see Ælfnóth and his son Ansgar," I said, and he led us toward the hall in the center of the *tún*.

They were waiting for us inside, Ælfnóth seated in his big chair on a raised platform at the end of the hearth, his *geréfa* standing to his right, and the recently penitent Ansgar to his left. I came directly to the point.

"I appeal Ansgar for the murder of the girl Eanswiðe and charge him to present himself for trial at the *gemót* after next."

"On what grounds?" Ælfnóth stood up and glowered down at me from his full height, augmented by the raised platform.

"On the grounds that he made the girl pregnant before the midsummer feast, and then refused to marry her, forcing her to either have his bastard or kill it to save her reputation. When he learned that she was going to abort the child, he killed her."

"That makes no sense at all," Ælfnóth snorted.

It was a theory cobbled together from bits of hearsay, certain observed facts, and coincidences, but that didn't mean it was wrong, or at least so far wrong that it wouldn't explain the girl's murder.

"I think it makes a kind of sense," I said. "What do you think, Benedict?"

The *mæsse-thegn*, hanging back as if he weren't entirely comfortable in Ælfnóth's house, seemed surprised to be consulted.

"The cunning woman is responsible for her death," the priest asserted.

"You said that before," I reminded him. "Have you discovered some factual proof since we last spoke?"

The *mæsse-thegn* was silent, in the baffling position of being contradicted by someone who didn't have to come to him for the sacraments and didn't believe in the infallibility of his innate knowledge. I also knew that my Latin pronunciation was at least as good as his, a fact that didn't bear on the matter at hand but made me feel better nonetheless.

"I'm wondering why you're even here."

"I am the shepherd of this flock," the *mæsse-thegn* said. "It is my place to protect my sheep from the false accusations of someone who—"

"Insists on proof?" I suggested.

"What proof do you have?"

"I have a dead girl who was carrying the bastard of someone who wouldn't marry her," I said. "Dead because she let her killer get close enough to stab her in the back. Dead because she was going to get rid of the bastard or make trouble if she didn't. Dead where she was learning wortcunning, a skill that you seem to have a particular hatred for. Dead on her back in a pool of blood but the front of her dress soaked with water.

"I have Ansgar upset and hurrying to the church where I found him making his confession to you. Ansgar with the leather of his bag and knife sheath and flask dark with water that must have been spilled out in a hurry. Ansgar who was known to be keeping company with the dead girl until just after the midsummer festival when they had an argument of some temperature. Ansgar who later had a less successful and even more heated argument with Ósmód that ended with him on his arse with a bloody nose.

"I have the dead girl wearing a bronze bracelet, but not long enough to stain her wrist the same color of green as Ansgar's wrist where a bronze bracelet used to be, and she's conveniently dead and hidden away in a place where she wouldn't be discovered until the ravens announced her—a place that would discredit someone you insist is responsible for her death. And I have a *mæsse-thegn* who knew she'd been stabbed before anyone told him how she'd died."

"Am I to have murdered her now?" The priest drew himself up and assumed the aggrieved expression of the wrongfully accused.

"No, you were pottering about the church all morning, just as you claimed when I asked you, seen in and out of there by half the village."

"What about Ósmód?" Ansgar said. "He came to the church covered in blood and he still is. He's been after Eanswiðe since they were children."

"He was nutting lambs this morning and docking their tails, with witnesses who are just as bloody, but don't take my word for it, let's ask him."

"I was nutting lambs, like he says, but the advocate's got a lot of it right. Eanswiðe told me she was carrying your bastard and you were going to let her because she was a *ceorl* and good enough to fock but not good enough to marry. I told her to keep the baby and I'd marry her, but she never loved me like I loved her, and she said she wouldn't marry someone she didn't love. I told her to appeal you for rape at the *gemót*."

"He was jealous," Ansgar said in a tone that seemed desperate to me. "He killed her because she wouldn't marry him."

"I'd be inclined to think you might be right except for all those witnesses working with him in the shearing barn and that bucket of lamb's balls, which apparently fry up nice and tasty if you peel and slice them and dip them in egg yolk and bread crumbs and throw them on a griddle with fresh rosemary and a spoonful of tallow. Makes me hungry just to think of it. I think we can excuse Ósmód from suspicion.

"You, on the other hand, were seen running up the hill to church, like you were coming from below the village, not running down the hill like you would if you were coming from

the *tún*. What was it you were running to confess with such penitential haste, I wonder?"

"This is all coincidence," the *mæsse-thegn*
said. "You sneer at what I know in my heart to
be true and claim you learned better at the
minster school in Eoforwic, but all you have to
offer as proof are disconnected things you put
together any way it suits you."

"I learned something else at the minster
school," I said with confidence. "There was a
physician there called Beanburh, who taught us
anatomy. He was a grouchy old fart, but he'd
been the doctor to the king and the archbishop
since before I was born, and we used to try to
divert him from his lessons, which were dry
and boring to young boys. Once he told us how
a murdered man's eyes hold the image of his
killer. Perhaps we should all walk down into the
village and look into Eanswiðe's eyes to see the
face of the last person she saw before she died.
Who do you think it will be?"

Ansgar's nerve broke at that suggestion, and
he started sniveling. His father, who'd seemed
willing to insist on his son's innocence to the
end, stepped away from him as if he were a
stranger, his eyes open in surprise. It's always a
disappointment to discover you don't know
someone as well as you thought.

"Eanswiðe was going to kill the child,"
Ansgar choked out. "My son would have gone
to the limbo of infants for eternity, and
Eanswiðe would have gone to hell for murder. I
did it so I could baptize the baby and it could
go to God innocent of original sin, and she

could die without murder on her soul."

"So to a certain way of thinking about it, slipping that knife in her back was really a piece of mercy."

"Yes," he said. "I gave her my bronze arm ring that she always liked and put my arms around her and hugged her and told her she was doing the right thing, and she never saw it coming. She wasn't afraid at all."

That wasn't my impression when I found her, but I didn't contradict him.

"And you confessed the murder and were forgiven," I said.

Ansgar nodded, relieved that I recognized the purity of his motive.

I looked at the *mæsse-thegn*. The theological afterlife is divided into four parts: hell for the damned, heaven for the elect, the limbo of the patriarchs for good men who must be cleansed of their sins before they can stand before God, and the limbo of infants who die unbaptized, unforgiven of Original Sin, and who therefore can never share the beatific vision. If you ask people at random what happens after you die, most of them will tell you that you go to heaven or hell. A few cynical sots who think they're witty will tell you that you're food for the worms. A very few who remember their catechism might dredge up the idea of limbo to atone for any sins you didn't have the opportunity to confess, but almost no one will mention the limbo of infants. That's the kind of subtle distinction they like to spend hours chewing on in places where they also teach perfect Latin pronunciation. I reckoned in the whole hundred there were no more than half a dozen men who weren't priests who'd even heard of it, and bad luck for Benedict, one of them was standing in Ælfnóth's hall listening to his son confess murder.

"Where did you hear about the limbo of infants?"

Ansgar stopped sobbing and looked momentarily confused, glancing at the *mæsse-thegn* before he could prevent himself.

"The seal of confession binds both the confessor and the confessed," the *mæsse-thegn* said. "Things discussed in confession can never be spoken of."

The *mæsse-thegn* Benedict was a slippery eel. I got to thinking about his initial accusation that the cunning woman had probably stabbed Eanswiðe, and, when he backed off from that, his repeated insistence that the cunning woman was certainly responsible for the murder. That was the sort of thinly sliced distinction that only made sense if he blamed Heregyð not for the actual murder but for its necessity. Why would he think she'd made the murder necessary? Maybe because it was the only way he could think of to be rid of her competition, unable to discredit her in the village where she'd grown up. I'd never know for sure, now that he'd reminded Ansgar to keep his mouth shut about the inconvenient details of his confessional council. Ansgar didn't seem like a man who'd come up with an idea that complicated without benefit of pastoral guidance.

Ansgar wasn't the first weak-willed man *in extremis* who'd been manipulated into a murder, and he wouldn't be the last, but I was having one of those moments of pure knowledge that the *mæsse-thegn* was so familiar with, and what I knew, and knew I could never prove, was that the whole point of Eanswiðe's murder hadn't been for Ansgar to be rid of Eanswiðe and the costly unpleasantness that comes of getting a bastard on a *ceorl*, it had been to rid the *mæsse-thegn* of Heregyð, whose herbal potions were more effective than his prayers for treating the flux.

"Ansgar denied the killing," I said to Ælfnóth. "An unannounced killing is murder, and beyond composition. But I can't see how anyone benefits by hanging Ansgar. It won't restore a living daughter to Æsc and Leola or an apprentice to Heregyð. It will deprive you of a son and your son of his life. The *wergeld* for killing a *ceorl* is two hundred shillings, for a pregnant woman one and one half times the usual *geld*. And her apprenticeship to the cunning woman adds another hundred shillings. If you're willing to compose the killing with four hundred shillings, I'm willing to treat his confession as an announcement and appeal him for manslaughter instead of murder."

Ælfnóth looked at his son with disgust and consulted with his *tún geréfa*. While they were conferring I stepped over to the *mæsse-thegn*.

"*Mæsse-thegns* know about guilt," I said. "It's your stock in trade. I first learned about it in the minster in Eoforwic, and for a long time I thought that what I learned there was the whole of what there is to know about it, but when I went to work in the *gemót* courts I quick discovered that there's a difference between legal guilt and moral guilt. The priest who taught me about guilt at Eoforwic liked to say that there are degrees of it attached to an act, so that the hand that holds the knife may be guilty of a killing, but the man who puts the knife in that man's hand, or the idea of the killing in that man's mind, is far from innocent himself.

"Now, bastards like you are protected by Canon Law," I went on in a low voice. "And we both know the likelihood of conviction if I appealed you to an ecclesiastical court on grounds of moral guilt. As it happens, I know archbishop Eanbald, and he's the sort of man who'd insist on proof instead of just taking my word for what I know in my heart to be true. We both know how frustrating that can be. But gossip is a corrosive thing in a village. And no matter how perfectly you speak your Latin when you say mass, I think your welcome here is going to be somewhat cold from now on. If I were you I'd think about finding another parish."

The *mæsse-thegn* looked at me like I was something disgusting he'd found on the bottom of his boot after a walk through a pasture and then turned and left the hall. Heregyð watched him leave and then took Ósmód's hand and led him down the length of the hearth to wait for us by the door. Eawa was watching Ansgar, who was watching his father and the *tún geréfa* decide if it was fiscally prudent to keep his third son from the gallows.

"So this is how the law works in Elmet," Eawa said.

"This is how it works today."

"Did that old priest Beanburh really teach you that you can see the killer's face in a murdered man's eyes?" Eawa asked.

"He told us it was a common belief," I admitted with a smile. "But he said he'd looked into enough dead eyes to know that it was just a load of shite, however many people might think it's true. There's nothing in a dead man's eyes but death."

hangeling

In those first days   my father and mother
left me for dead: there was no life yet,
no life within me.

Riddle 20, Exeter Book

Driffield, Northumbria 786

1 **τ sτarτed snowing** late in the
morning, at first nothing more than soft
fluff, like the down of a snow goose drifting in the air currents, swirling around and
never seeming to come to rest. It was easy to
think that the snow wasn't settling because the
gradually darkening ground was still warm
enough to melt it, and we pressed on toward
the royal *ville* at Driffield, as the ground sof-
tened with the snowmelt and the hard dirt underfoot turned to slick mud, because we had
business there that had to be concluded before
Yule.

We were three or four hours on the road when the cart suddenly skidded sideways and one of the wheels dropped into the rut, which popped the axle out of alignment. The cart shuddered and wobbled against the shafts and threw the horse off what passed for its already debilitated stride. We unhitched and unloaded our gear so we could turn the cart on its side and fix the axle brace. By the time we'd repaired the brace and reloaded the cart and started again, the temperature had dropped below freezing and chilly white dust was collecting on the dry stalks of heath grass and the dwarf gorse.

"It's colder," Banta said. There was a grease smear across his forehead and cheek, and I'd decided not to tell him about it. Petty amusement is a low form of amusement, but it was cold, and the day had already been disrupted sufficiently that we might have to spend another night outside before we got to Driffield. I was taking my amusement where I found it.

"Ground's still warm," I said.

"Only means it'll get muddier before it hardens," he complained. "If we don't keep moving the wheels will freeze into the mud."

I could always count on Banta to put an optimistic spin on things.

After another mile or two the snowflakes got bigger and fell harder, and the visible world closed in on us. It was like that for another hour, and then that first, semi-transparent layer of snowflakes that had collected on the ground became opaque, the colors underneath still faintly visible, and then they faded away and there was only the unbroken white everywhere you looked. The flakes swirled around us, and the trees became faint shapes beside the road. Snow collected on the flat surfaces of the cart and our gear and the shafts on either side of the horse and on the horse's head and back.

The horse shook itself feebly every couple of steps it took and, its breath erupting from its nostrils in two smoky plumes as it walked, bobbed its head like it was going to fall over in the traces. I didn't pay any attention because it walked like that most of the time. The horse had no name, in keeping with Banta's insistence that animals were just tools and naming them made it harder when they died. The horse had looked like it was on the verge of death ever since I'd encountered it four winters before, and it was still hanging on, refusing to die so we could replace it with another nameless horse.

It was mid- or late-afternoon, but in the eddying snow it was difficult to estimate; the light was dim and blue and changeless. I couldn't tell where the sun was in the sky. I pulled my cloak tighter around my shoulders. It was like walking in some strange limbo of suspended time. Banta was superstitious, susceptible to worry about elfshot, and I knew he'd start to get anxious before long. He liked to be able to see what was coming from a distance. The *weald* is a dangerous place on a sunny day in Ærra Líða; in a freezing blizzard on the second day of Ærra Jéola it's even more dangerous.

We stopped to rest the horse and have a

piss, standing with our backs to the direction we thought the wind was coming from, shoulder to shoulder beside the cart while we made steaming, yellow holes in the snow.

"How much farther to the *ville*?" I asked.

"When we started out this morning we were fifteen Roman miles away, but in this snow it's hard to tell—it could be ten more Roman miles or it could be round the next bend in the road."

"Shite on a stick. Are you considering how nice it would be to have a waggon big enough to climb into out of the snow and a real horse to pull it instead of a dung cart and this nag?"

"No."

There was something disturbing about the storm, but not because there was howling wind driving icy snowflakes into our exposed flesh like a thousand sharpened clamshells, flitching the skin off our faces. It was disturbing because the snow was everywhere and nowhere, spiraling and falling down, up, sideways—circling in frigid vortices. Limbo would be like this, if limbo existed, so cold it felt hot, and you alone with your thoughts in eternal white isolation. You could close your eyes and breathe deeply, like inhaling needles of ice, and hold your burning breath in your lungs and listen to the snow brush your ears, and believe that nothing existed but you and the cold, or ever would again.

Banta stroked the horse's neck, muttering something to it. The horse stood with a drooped head, looking like it hoped the day would end in a warm dry place where it could die in comfort and have it all over with. In the cart, the ferrets in the covered wicker cage were gathered into a compact pile for warmth and the fyste dogs were huddled together in the corner of the cart bed.

A sound swelled out of the snow, swirling among the flakes—louder, softer—and faded away. I looked around, but visibility was down to only a few feet, directionless—without a sense of up or down I felt as if I'd float away. Banta and the horse were outlines, sometimes smudges, like they were standing behind sheer gauze. The sound was gone—only the whispering of the storm. I listened, trying to parse the layers of frozen stillness.

I shook the snow off my hood and listened again. The snow sounded like a length of silk slowly drawn across starched linen. It sounded like a breath held in anticipation of something I didn't want to think about. Then I heard the sound again—faint, not so faint, rising, falling, disintegrating.

"Did you hear that?"

"What?"

Banta was alert. He reached up with both hands and flared the hood on either side of his head and slowly turned at the waist to scan the area in front of him and collect any sound. He was cautious about sounds he couldn't place in context. Those kinds of sounds are frequently trouble, sometimes dangerous.

Then there was a sharp hiccup of a cry in an urgent rhythm, a gasp of breath followed by another cry, another gasp, then another cry.

Banta might not recognize it, being childless, but I was the veteran of many a bare-assed walk beside the cooling hearth to see what was wrong with a crying child, and I knew the source of the cry immediately.

"It's a baby," I said, turning my head in an attempt to fix the location.

We stepped to opposite sides of the road, but the sound was gone.

"Get one of the dogs," he said.

The snow made that crisp, sharp crunch under my feet when I walked to the back of the cart and picked a dog out of the pile. There were low growls as I disturbed them, and then they repositioned themselves, became a struggling scrum as they jockeyed to occupy any warmth abandoned by the dog I'd taken. I carried the dog to Banta and handed it to him. Banta was the one who liked dogs. I don't mind dogs; they have their uses, but I prefer cats and ferrets to the small unpleasant fystes, which seem to me like some kind of monstrous rat themselves.

Banta held the dog against his chest and the three of us listened. Then the cry came on the wind again, and the dog cocked its head. Banta set it on the ground and it started pushing through the snow—already shoulder high on the little ratting terrier. We followed the broken furrow into the whiteout. The dog never wavered, ploughing straight toward the baby that was out there somewhere crying in the blizzard.

Not more than a few rods into the vaporous heath there was a small stone cairn, mottled with lichen, and looming over it the desiccated and blasted stump of what had once been a big oak, overturned so its roots twisted into the sky like the fingers of a dead, arthritic hand. In a crevice under the gnarled roots we found a small bundle, swaddled and wrapped in a dirty fleece. It had probably been warm when it was placed under the stump, maybe asleep, then the snow had started to fall, and the air had gotten colder; maybe it shat itself or pissed in the fleece, warm at first, not that uncomfortable, and then the wet cold that kept getting colder.

The baby didn't seem more than a day or two old. Banta and I exchanged a look. If it had been born today, it had been born on *Frigedæg*, the day that was considered to be the unluckiest day of the week to be born. Given its current situation that would make sense.

"One too many mouths," he said.

I nodded.

Many families, faced with another mouth in lean times, made the hard decision to leave a newborn to take its chance with Fate in the form of a wolf or a wild hog or a bear or the kindness of any stranger who might discover it before the beasts did. Unbaptized, unnamed, defenseless, perhaps unwanted and unloved, the baby squirmed and turned its wrinkled face to the side and wailed in discomfort.

I'd found the remains of exposed children before, usually only gnawed bones cracked for their marrow or swaddles stiff with dried blood and shite and the elemental abuse of the open air. I'd never found an exposed baby alive, so

I'd never had a choice to make. I looked at Banta.

"Is there a convent nearby?"

"Not that I know of," he said. "And if there is, who's to say it didn't come from there?"

"Well, I can't walk away from it."

"I didn't think you could," he said in a tone that implied that *he* could, and probably would have done if he'd discovered it by himself. "You don't think it's a changeling, do you?"

Like many people, Banta's a believer in elves. Now, as a former believer in a deity that's supposed to have both a human and a divine nature and was incarnated by a virgin birth, who was I to judge him? In his great work, *Apeiros*, Parmenides of Elea posited the idea of an infinite universe; and in an infinite universe isn't anything possible, including elves and the existence of a deity that made his entrance into the phenomenological world from between a virgin's thighs? Maybe. But we all have to draw the line somewhere.

Elves are thought to steal human babies and replace them with their own so that they can suckle on human milk, which for some reason elves consider to be a delicacy, but this can only be done before the human baby is baptized. What then? Why change out a perfectly healthy elvish baby for an unwanted human baby abandoned on a heath in a blizzard? *Cui bono?* Searching for logic in belief is a waste of time.

"I doubt it's a changeling," I said.

The fyste was sniffing at the baby. Banta shifted it away with his foot and stooped to pick up the bundle. The baby stopped wailing when he lifted it into the air, and it looked around wide-eyed, a surprised, red moon face surrounded by tangled fleece—amazed to be floating in the snowy air.

"If you're not a changeling, then what are you doing out here?" Banta asked. "Looking for trouble?"

The fyste circled tight around Banta's ankles, the stump of its docked tail jerking spasmodically from side to side.

"Have we got any milk?"

"There might be a little sheep's milk," I said. "Probably frozen. We'll need to warm it up, anyway."

"Let's not waste any time, then."

We turned away from the stump and started to follow our trail back toward the road. The cart was invisible in the falling snow. The fyste hopped ahead of us, yapping and dancing excitedly, and then it stopped dead in its tracks and looked into the whiteness. After a moment it gave a sudden fearful yelp and ran back to cower at Banta's feet. We stopped walking and peered into the snow, drawing our *seaxes*. Whatever had scared the fyste was out there, maybe twenty yards away, maybe fifty, maybe just five or ten feet, beyond our visible range. After a few tense moments an indistinct shadow materialized out of the swirling flakes, standing about ten yards away looking at us. It was a large wolf. It must have been attracted by the baby's cries and smell and come to investigate. I hoped it was alone.

It stood stiller than stillness itself while it watched us for a moment and then dematerialized into the whiteness without moving. It had appeared and disappeared the way wolves appear and disappear all the time. We hurried the rest of the way back to the cart.

The horse was standing there shivering, two or three deep breaths away from dropping dead in the harness—so, the usual. The fyste jumped into the cart and burrowed into the pile of rat dogs, as if that would keep it safe from the wolf. The fact that it could probably smell the wolf out there in the blizzard was doing nothing to settle its nerves. Banta nodded for me to open the ferret cage. I brushed the accumulated snow from the canvas cover into the bed of the cart and lifted it away from the cage so I could open the hinged top. The ferrets were sleeping in a nest of straw and rags and not best pleased to be disturbed by the cold draft. Banta lowered the baby into the cage and nestled it among the ferrets. They repositioned themselves around the fleece and draped themselves over the baby's form. If the baby started squalling again and woke the ferrets, it was on its own. Banta closed the top of the cage and replaced the canvas.

"We've got to shelter someplace we can make a fire," he said. "There must be a village somewhere close to hand."

I walked around to the horse's head and pulled on the bridle. Even with the motivating knowledge that there was a wolf nearby, at first it refused to move, it just swayed forward with the force of my pull, then it took a reluctant step and the cart lurched ahead. I walked beside the horse and Banta walked behind the cart, listening, I suppose, for sounds from the ferret cage and making sure the wolf didn't come up behind us. The baby was quiet.

Stories of infant exposure appear occasionally in Greek and Roman literature, often concerning someone who grows up to be a hero. I always reckoned it was one of those character-building literary devices meant to introduce the sort of adversity that would toughen the little mite up for the shitestorms of adult life and explain his eventual success. Oedipus and Paris had both survived exposure in the mountains. One of them killed his father and married his mother; the other one set the events into motion that ultimately caused the fall of Troy. The infants Romulus and Remus had been exposed in a tub and set afloat in the Tiber. That turned out a little better. Suckled by a she wolf, fed by a woodpecker, they grew up on the hilly riverbank and the town they founded eventually became Rome. Of course, when they were grown, Romulus killed Remus in a real estate dispute, but their descendants founded the greatest empire in the history of the world, so there was that.

There was one important story of infant exposure in the bible—Moses set adrift in a rush basket in the Nile like a tasty appetizer for the first crocodile to swim by. Lucky little Moses was discovered by the Pharaoh's daughter instead and grew up to lead the enslaved

Hebrews out of Egypt and deliver the Ten Commandments. Sounds a success story, doesn't it? But while they were wandering in the desert Moses found himself stuck between a carping mob of parched, ungrateful Israelites and a notoriously thin-skinned Old Testament God. When Yahweh told him to strike the rock with his staff to release the life-giving waters at Meribah, Moses muddled his instructions and made the mistake of striking the rock twice, which offended Yahweh's sense of divine Self-Importance. He interpreted that second strike as a lack of faith and the petulant old bush burner wouldn't let Moses into the Promised Land. Infant exposure might toughen you up, but it didn't always guarantee a good outcome.

In the real world, where exposure isn't a literary device inflicted on future heroes, messianic leaders, and the founders of empires to emphasize their humble origins, it hardly ever works out well for the baby. Even if we managed to find shelter, the baby's chances of living out the night weren't good. We had no way to feed it, for one thing. And if it lived to see morning, then what? I couldn't see us altruistically raising a child, like longsuffering but comically mismatched foster parents in some mythic foundation story, cheerfully enduring hardship to nurture a hero who'd grow up to become the *Bretwalda*, unify the kingdoms of Britain, and usher in a golden age. That's just not how it works. I thought the baby's best chance of survival was if we could find a convent. The church was usually willing to take in children, and nuns are widely known to be suckers for newborn babies.

Walking on frozen, rutted dirt was painful, and it was hard to know where the edge of the road was. The wheel ruts rocked the cart, and the baby, warmed by the ferrets and padded by the fleece and the straw, stayed quiet. It was just one foot in front of the other, without any sense of progress—floating snow in all directions, white in all directions, cold in all directions. The only sound was the creak of the cart and the crunch of the horse's hooves and our steps on the frozen, snow-covered road.

We seemed to trudge for hours without arriving at a village. I don't know how far we walked after we found the baby before a shadow finally congealed out of the whiteness and a little cluster of buildings took shape on our right—a small house, a couple of sheds. Then another cluster to our left, a little farther on. The smells of the place were sharp in the cold: hearth smoke, shite, unwashed people, cattle, and the overwhelming stink of swine. The smells of something cooking. My stomach rumbled and then quivered and turned over like it might reject the little that was in it.

The village was just a scatter of habitation; I reckoned no more than six or eight families, not even a complete tithing. The holdings were defined by wicker fencing around gardens and along the dirt paths that meandered off the main village street, snow-drifted now; there were no tracks but our own—everyone was hunkering inside piling wood on the fire, trying not to freeze. There was a large building located close to the center of the village and not in proximity to any houses that we took for a communal barn or stable. We looked inside and discovered half an ox team and their harness, yokes, plough, hoes, shovels, flails, sickles and scythes—all the tools and apparatus of field-work.

There was a small, soot-darkened stone hearth full of cold ash and memories of past fires, but there was no wood by the hearth and we needed a fire in the present. The cracks in the wall let in thin streams of cold air and although the stable offered us some shelter from the blizzard we weren't going to sleep comfortably unless we built a fire, and probably not then. It was only a matter of time before the baby woke up wailing with hunger and then died.

We carried the ferret cage inside and the dogs followed us, nosing around the stable to get a sense of what they were sharing it with and whether any of it was edible. The four oxen, cold but placid in their stalls, weren't overly upset by our arrival. Banta unhitched the horse and stabled him with the oxen. I forked some fodder into the manger and broke the ice on the water trough. The rich bovine smell of the stable reminded me of my sister's son, Ordgar. His father was a breeder and trainer of oxen and Ordgar had worked around them all his life, so his clothing was permeated with the same smell.

Banta threw a blanket over the horse, and

we carried the rest of our gear into the stable so it wouldn't be buried under snow. We always kept a little bit of firewood in the cart. Short lengths of branch and split sections of log have an amazing utility when it comes to getting a cart unstuck from the mud or chocking the wheels or clubbing a rat to death or, as in this case, building a fire for warmth. After I struck sparks into a handful of crushed straw I positioned the ferret cage close to the flames.

"I'll go find the *geréfa*," Banta said, pulling his cloak tighter and raising his hood again. "Make a deal." Then he was outside in a creak of wood and a cold blast of air, though it was barely colder than the temperature of the stable. What little wood we had wasn't going to last; I hoped he didn't forget to get more.

I opened the top of the cage and looked inside through the fog of my breath. The ferrets had arranged themselves around and over the baby so it looked like the baby was covered by a ferret blanket—a round face and two wide-open blue eyes staring up at me, probably wondering what the fock was going on. Ferrets sleep ten to fifteen hours at a time, but when they're awake they're as energetic as a burning bishop, so I knew that I'd have to get the baby out of there when the ferrets woke up. We generally played with them for an hour or two every day unless we were working them, in which case they got plenty of exercise and diversion down in a warren or inside the walls of a granary. When they woke up they'd be hungry and curious about their new cage mate and they'd want to play.

We had half a dozen frozen squirrels, snared yesterday; the ferrets would stay occupied trying to chew them up. For Banta and me there was some cheese and sausage and a hard loaf of bread. For the baby there was whatever we managed to beg from the women who lived in the village. With any luck we'd find a wet nurse willing to suckle the infant; in case we didn't, I set the bottle with the sheep's milk on the edge of the hearth to thaw and then warm before I tried to feed the baby. If the village had a cow it was sleeping somewhere else.

I checked the horse one more time. The animal looked like it was staring into a future of mortality and woe and the sweet release of death was its only hope, and that hope cruelly denied. It looked like it always looked. I went back to the hearth and checked the baby, which seemed to be still trying to puzzle out how it had come to be buried in ferrets, and then I stretched out on the ground close to the fire, wrapped in my cloak. It was quiet in the stable, horse and oxen motionless in the stalls, the dogs lying together for warmth, the baby and the ferrets in the cage. I looked at the cage, pulled close to the fire for the warmth, and wondered what that baby must be thinking of its day so far. I took a breath and closed my eyes.

It turns out dying, for all the fuss and struggle and dread, isn't that difficult, even if there's no one to help you along. It's just a matter of deciding that you've had enough of living. I was wrapped tight in a fleecy shroud, my arms and legs compressed and restrained, with only my face exposed to the cold, as if I were cocooned in a spider's web, aware and waiting for the stinging bite that would start to digest me before I died.

My field of vision was restricted in the near distance by the rocky edge of the niche I was lying in and closer still by the fleece hood; spinning flakes brushed my eyelashes and nose as they danced across my face. My cheeks stung with the cold. I made a squirming attempt to relieve the pressure of the point of rock that was digging into my back.

I don't know how long I was there, but at some point I started to feel the cold seeping through the fleece, drawing closer to the center of me with every breath, and how tired I was and how easy it would be to close my eyes and drift away on one of the snowflakes, which seemed large and substantial enough to bear the weight of my exhausted soul into the unknowable whiteness.

Then a shape coalesced out of the swirling white and a head filled the opening in the rocks. Thick fur in a symmetrically patterned mask of grey and brown, a white muzzle that ended in a black nose; the yellow eyes behind the mask drilled into the cold center of me. I took a deep breath to scream and filled my chest with icy air and I heard a high-pitched wail and then my throat and chest spasmed and I coughed and then I wailed again and cried. The wolf didn't react, it just watched me with those yellow eyes, then it looked to its left and its head disappeared back into the whiteness. I cried again as loudly as I could. A mist of exhaled breath floated briefly in front of my eyes and then melted into the drifting snow.

Then there was a small canine face sniffing warily at the edges of the rock crevice, ugly and angular like a tiny dog skull covered with short fur stretched so tight over the bone that it made the eyes bulge. Then it was replaced by two bearded faces looking into the rock crevice from a great height, beards a tangle of steaming, ice-coated bristles. One of them reached toward me and I was lifted suddenly out of the shelter of the rocks into the swirling snow and he said...

"Hring. Wake up."

I opened my eyes and blinked in the dim red light of the smoky fire.

Banta stood in the door for a moment and then stepped into the stable. The draft made the flames quiver back to transitory life. The light outside was dimmer but still directionless, light coming from everywhere at once. I must have dozed and dreamed what the baby had experienced before we found it. The wood in the center of the fire had been consumed and there were smoking spokes radiating from where the flames had been. I reached over and pushed the unburned ends of the sticks and logs toward the coals in the center, and after a moment the fire blazed up again. Banta was still standing to the side of the open door, waiting for someone to follow him into the stable, and then he closed the door. We'd achieved a quorum now: the three wise men.

I thought it was probably the *geréfa*. Village *geréfas* are responsible for knowing who's in their jurisdiction and why. Our first bit of business when we come to a village is always to make ourselves known to the *geréfa*. Strangers are dangerous ciphers to be explained in some knowable way or moved along without ceremony. A man without land or local relationships has nothing to lose—the law has little or no hold over him; a stranger can be a thief or a killer, unconstrained by allegiance or relationship and consequently beyond control. When no one's responsible for your *frith-borh*, you're responsible to no one, and men who are responsible to no one are often willing to do anything.

We'd worked for many churches and monastic foundations, and when we were in the territory of a bishop or abbot we knew we would often invoke his name as the guarantor of our *frith-borh*, and most of the time that was enough, but not infrequently we had to demonstrate our *bona fides* in some way, often by killing a few rats for free. This was more impressive to the locals than it would have been if they'd known that we didn't depend on the profit from killing rats to live. Banta and I work for Offa's spymaster, Brorda, and killing rats is only our cover, not our livelihood. We're spies and *cwalu-thegnan*.

Brorda was a skinflint who expected us to support ourselves exterminating rats, but if we had a run of bad ratting luck or there was some emergency, coin caches were scattered around the countryside, troves of silver from which Brorda's agents could make withdrawals if the need arose. So while our apparently reckless generosity in agreeing to work for free might impress the yokels, it was all for show and to ingratiate us with the *geréfa*.

But as soon as the man pushed his hood back, I knew he wasn't the village *geréfa*, unless it was the fashion in these parts for *geréfas* to wear a tonsure. He was young and awkward, with big ears sticking out from his head, bright red with cold, and wide blue eyes. His hair was cut raggedly at the base of his neck and chopped straight across his forehead. He was wearing thick wool mittens and had a leather bag hanging over one shoulder. I marked him for a man not that long away from wherever he'd trained to be a priest, inexperienced and probably insecure in his position.

"This is Eldlyn," Banta said. "The village *masse-thegn*."

Banta had an armload of firewood, and he dropped it beside the hearth. The clatter was loud in the stable, and the oxen shifted position, crowding our horse. The horse released a sequential plopping of steaming road apples in protest.

"Terrible night," I said. You can't go wrong starting out with a comment about the weather.

"Have you been on the road long?"

"All day. Held up by cart trouble this morning. We're heading to the royal *ville* at Driffield."

"Then you've arrived."

"This is Driffield?"

"It is."

"We must have gotten turned around in the storm," I said to Banta. "I didn't realize we'd come so far."

"How much farther to the *ville*?" Banta asked the priest. "This is our first time here."

"It's a mile farther north," Eldlyn said.

"Have you been here long?"

"I came last summer to found the parish of Saint Mary at the site of king Aldfrith's burial mound."

"We're hired to kill rats at the royal *ville* before Yule," Banta told him.

"Is the king coming for Yule?"

Banta shrugged his ignorance. "We just kill rats."

"Did you find the *geréfa*?" I asked.

"The *tún-geréfa* has jurisdiction over the village," Banta said. "And he's tucked in at the *ville* all nice and warm. We'll stay here tonight and go on to the *ville* tomorrow."

"Sorry to keep you from your dinner," I said to the *masse-thegn*.

"I was shriving a newborn," Eldlyn said. "I ran into Banta on my way back to the church."

Banta and I exchanged a glance.

"A newborn?" Shriving means hearing confession and absolving sins. It was a remarkable newborn if it had sins to confess and words to confess them.

"I should say a stillborn," Eldlyn emended. "Died as it left its mother's womb with the cord

169

round its neck. I baptized it and blessed it with chrism."

I had to admire Eldlyn's determination; making a pointless pastoral visit in a blizzard recommended his sense of duty. Baptizing a stillborn baby would save it from the Limbo of Infants and allow it to enter into heaven. I thought all of that was a load of shite, of course, but he didn't. Back when I did believe in such things, I thought the Limbo of Infants would be a lot like the weather outside, a timeless fog of cold white solitude in which the souls of infants were doomed to spend eternity alone, out of the presence of god. Like many things, the Church has a different take on infants than the secular world does. The *dóm-bócs* don't consider that infants even have souls until they quicken in the womb, and they aren't considered fully human under law until they're baptized and fed and have survived for forty days.

If we'd found the exposed baby back when I'd been a believer, and then heard about the stillborn in the village, I'd have jumped to the superstitious conclusion that somewhere in the snowy, indistinct whiteness of the heath we'd passed through the open gate of Limbo, and that we'd retrieved the soul of the dead baby and returned to the world before the gate closed, where it had coalesced into flesh and blood and nothing but trouble for us.

Fortunately, absent the encumbrance of belief in god, I could see it for what it was: bad luck for the dead baby and possibly good luck for the one that was still alive. But still a complicating trouble for us. We had an agenda at the royal *ville* that didn't include caring for a foundling.

"Did you tell him what we discovered on the road?" I asked Banta.

"Thought I'd show him."

"Show me what?"

Banta opened the top of the ferret cage and stepped back so the priest could look inside. Eldlyn had a quick glance and recoiled in surprise.

"Is that a baby?"

The first thing out of a surprised person's mouth is very often the stupidest thing they've said all day.

"We found it under an uprooted tree stump on a heath, miles from here."

"I know the place," Eldlyn said. "It's not so far away. That's where unwanted babies are exposed."

That explained the presence of the wolf. It wasn't just a coincidence. The blasted stump marked the location where inconvenient children were abandoned, and probably had done since the time of the Celts, but to the wolf it was just a feeding station. If we'd come to the place even ten minutes later the wolf would probably have already carried the baby back to its den, and not to suckle it so it could grow up to become the *Bretwalda*.

Eldlyn made the sign of the cross and said a prayer. I applied myself to building up the fire. Our exhaled breath was foggy in the stable, and it would have to be a lot warmer before I took the baby out of the ferret cage to examine it. If it was deformed in some way there was little hope that even a convent full of sentimental nuns would be willing to raise it, and we'd just prolonged its life needlessly. There was also the problem of feeding it, and I don't mean just finding a couple of tits full of milk.

Under law, newborns aren't considered to be fully human; that's why the naming and the baptism are delayed for a couple of days. If you expose an unnamed, unbaptized baby, the law treats it as just an unfortunate birthing event, but the *dóm-bócs* consider the act of feeding an infant to be symbolic of your intention to raise it, and that act bestows human status on it. If you expose a baby after you've fed it, the law views your action the same as a murder. So if we fed the child, we were responsible for it, and if we couldn't find a convent or a foster parent, we were stuck with an unweaned infant until we could unload it on someone with the where-withal to keep it alive.

I picked up the bottle and shook it. There was a rattling slosh that indicated the milk was only partially thawed. I set the bottle in the ashes at the edge of the fire to speed up the process.

"Have you examined it for the devil's mark?"

"Didn't want to unswaddle it in the cold."

The *masse-thegn* nodded, but I could see him looking around for some flat surface. Eldlyn wanted to verify that the infant hadn't been claimed by Satan in the womb or found by elves who'd substituted a changeling before he proceeded any further. There was no point in trying to talk sense to him; he was going to do what he was going to do. Eldlyn repositioned a short bench beside the ferret cage and drew up a small barrel for a seat and started to reach into the cage, hesitated, and looked at me.

"Will the ferrets bite?"

"Christ in a velvet gown," Banta grunted impatiently and shouldered the *masse-thegn* aside. He thrust both hands into the cage and redistributed the pile of ferrets and then lifted the baby free. The baby was surprised to be lifted from the warm covering of ferrets, and it started squalling. Banta handed the swaddled baby to the *masse-thegn*.

The priest took the baby and laid it on the bench. He undid the knot in the leather thong that secured the sheepskin and opened the thick outer covering, then peeled away the swaddling.

"Well, does it have a tail or hooves?" Banta's impatience was showing through. "Because if it does, no wonder they put it under that stump."

Banta was a past master at saying something in a tone that the listener could interpret however he wanted. The priest no doubt thought that he was serious, but I knew he was mocking the whole business although, as a believer in elves, I knew if the priest discovered something that pointed in that direction Banta really would consider putting the baby back where we found it.

"That wasn't the reason," Eldlyn said after a moment's scrutiny. He leaned back from the squirming baby, so we could see that it was a boy, but we could also see that whoever had swaddled him had included a fold of linen cloth. The priest unfolded the cloth in his palm. A polished silver penny glistened in the red light, but he was more interested in the cloth than the coin, and he closed his fingers over the penny and held the cloth up for us to see. In the center of the square of linen was an embroidered likeness of a crowned man holding a scepter.

"This is king Aldfrith," he said. "I'm the custodian of his mound and shrine, and there's a slave woman lives at the royal *ville* makes these for me."

Aldfrith was the king who'd followed his older brother Ecgfrith to the throne after Ecgfrith and his army had been wiped out by the Picts at Nechtansmere a hundred years ago. Northumbria had been the foremost kingdom in Britain, but ever since Ecgfrith's brother Ælfwine, his sub-king in Diera, had his arse handed to him by the Mercians in the Trent valley six years before that, Northumbria had ceded its supremacy to Mercia, and Ecgfrith had been struggling to maintain his hold over Northern Britain. Against all sensible advice and the attempts of his friend Bishop Cuthberht of Lindisfarne to discourage him, Ecgfrith took his army north to subdue the Picts before he turned his attention to the Mercians, but those sneaky Picts lured him onto unfavorable ground beside a highland loch, and he suddenly discovered himself in the middle of a massacre, just like his brother before him, except that his army was being cut to pieces by half-naked wild men who'd painted themselves blue and worked themselves into a battle frenzy to the screeching wail of highland pipes instead of inartistic, overdressed midlands thugs who worked unimaginatively without the benefit of musical accompaniment.

Aldfrith had been consigned to the Church, as the youngest brothers in royal kindreds frequently are, and he was living on Iona, the holy island to the west that had been the base from which the Celtic Church had launched the conversion of Northumbria. He'd been pursuing a quiet life of contented monkish scholarship and prayer when his brother led his army into the disastrous highlands shitestorm, and when word of it reached Eoforwic, the Northumbrian *witan* sent a delegation to bring his reluctant, tonsured arse back to assume the throne. The Church must have thought that God himself had arranged the bloodbath at Nechtansmere to get rid of hard-headed Ecgfrith and replace him with his much more pliable brother, who was used to taking orders from superior Churchmen and as biddable to their will as a first year novice.

Aldfrith became a good king to the Northumbrians and, as you'd expect, enjoyed good relations with the Church, except for bishop Wilfrið, as you'd also expect—no one got along with Wilfrið. Aldfrith had been raised in the rites and traditions of the Celtic Church, and Wilfrið was the man whose arguments at the big synod at Streanshalch had ensured the primacy of the Roman Church that resulted in the expulsion of the Celtic-rite priests. Aldfrith and Wilfrið were like a cat and a dog sewn together into a small sack and dropped in the river. Northumbria wasn't big enough for the two of them, and since Wilfrið had made a career out of alienating every other bishop in Britain, there was no one to support him when Aldfrith finally had enough of his shite and banished him from the kingdom.

In my opinion, that act alone was sufficient to qualify Aldfrith for elevation to sainthood, the requisite number of miracles could always be discovered later; but the sad fact is that no one in Rome agreed with me, sensitive as they tend to be about the Episcopal prerogative, even when their bishops are flaming arseholes, so despite a cult following and a partisan minority among the Northumbrian faithful who lobbied for his sanctity, and however good a reputation he'd enjoyed in life, Aldfrith was just another dead Northumbrian king, and Wilfrið was the saint.

The fact that the *masse-thegn* was the keeper of Aldfrith's shrine and burial mound and had a sideline in embroidered likenesses of the king to sell to the gullible pilgrims who came to his grave was an interesting coincidence that had allowed him to tentatively identify the origin of the baby.

"The baby was born to someone on the royal *ville*?"

"To the woman who made this. Her name is Eithne. She's a Pict from the far north."

"Why expose the bairn? They've plenty to eat on a royal *ville*."

"Because the father's the prefect, and his wife doesn't want her husband's bastard to grow up in the same household as her legitimate children."

The laws concerning the status of children born to slaves are complicated but not obscure. If a woman's pregnant at the time she's enslaved, the child's freeborn because the mother was free when the child was conceived. If she becomes pregnant after she's enslaved, then the child might or might not be a slave, depending on whether the father's a free man or another slave. If he's a free man, then the child's free. If the father's a slave; the child's a slave.

If the prefect was really the baby's father, then, according to law, the baby we found on the heath was free because children inherit their father's status and class in society. But because his mother was a slave she had no say in what happened to the child, and the father, her owner, was within his paternal rights if he wanted to expose him, so long as he hadn't been fed.

"Did you know she was pregnant?"

Eldlyn nodded. "In a village this small, everyone knows everything. The prefect's wife hated seeing a big-bellied slave woman carrying her husband's bastard. But I didn't know they were going to do this."

"What's the problem?" Banta wanted to know. "You've a woman lost a child and a man who doesn't want one. Switch them and everyone's content."

"The baby wouldn't be safe if the prefect's wife knew it was alive. They could have sold it or given it away, but they wanted it gone for good."

"Was the dead baby a boy or a girl?"

"Boy."

"There you are. One baby looks like another except for what's between its legs," Banta said. "How would they know?"

Eldlyn shook his head and looked into the fire, but he'd stopped arguing that the deception wouldn't work. I thought it might be worth the attempt. The baby was crying now, naked in the cold air. We had to do something soon.

"Why not let the parents of the dead child decide?" I asked.

The *masse-thegn* considered it for a long moment and then stood up.

"I'll ask them."

"We'll come with you," I said. I walked over to the horse and pulled the blanket off its back. The horse looked around at me as if he wondered why I'd waited so long to increase his discomfort.

I saw a pair of shears hanging on a nail, and I took them down and cut a square out of the corner of the blanket. Considerate softie that I am, I shook out the square of wool to dislodge any lice or ticks. I thought the baby needed a change of costume if I was to successfully pass him off as a poor foundling ragamuffin. I lifted the baby by its feet and pushed the fleece onto the floor and set the baby back down on the rough wool. If he'd been squalling in discomfort before, when he was only naked and cold, rough wool scraping across his arse increased his displeasure by two or three orders of magnitude. I was fine with that. It wasn't any more of an inconvenience than the rest of his day so far, and I thought that holding a crying baby wrapped in a ragged horse blanket could only help our case when we pitched our plan to the grieving parents.

Banta and Eldlyn waited impatiently while I discarded the fleece and rolled the squirming baby into the blanket. The texture was scratchy as hell, but it must have retained a little warmth from the horse because the baby seemed to calm down when I was finished. I picked him up and cradled him in my left arm while I retrieved the fleece and the linen swaddles from the ground. Banta opened the door, and the *masse-thegn* walked outside, and I followed him.

"They live across the common on the far edge of the village," Eldlyn said, leading the way through the falling snow.

Banta and I walked close behind so we wouldn't lose sight of the *masse-thegn*. I'd noticed a pig sty on the way in, and I tossed the shite-smeared linen and the fleece over the stone wall, trusting the pigs, who'd think a square of linen seasoned with baby shite was manna from heaven, to consume all recognizable evidence of the foundling. Eldlyn led us through a little cluster of buildings, past some sunken houses, and across a wide, open expanse of ground. After half a dozen steps we couldn't see anything but Eldlyn's back, but another dozen paces brought us into a cluster of buildings, small sheds, a small, roofed structure without walls where they probably worked in the summer, and then to a wattle-and-daub house. Eldlyn walked up to the door and knocked on the boards. We stood a little distance behind him.

"It's Eldlyn."

After a moment the door opened a crack and a man looked out.

"Father?"

"I have to come in," he said. "There's something I want to ask you."

The man looked over his shoulder at me and Banta, wondering who we were and what we wanted.

"They're with me," the *masse-thegn* said. "They're part of it."

The man stepped aside and opened the door wide enough to let us in.

The interior of the house was much warmer than the stable had been. There was a fire burning hot and high in the hearth and the walls were hung with insulating hides. The thatch held the heat of the fire in the space under the roof, and it was comfortable. There was a little girl, about three winters old, sitting on the edge of the sleeping platform with a shawl around her shoulders, all big eyed and afraid of the death and the strangers in the house. A woman was lying on the platform under blankets and some fleeces that had been sewn together into an irregular comforter. She looked pale in the red firelight.

The man walked back to the platform and stood beside his wife.

"What do you want to ask?"

"This is Banta and Hring," he said. "They're ratcatchers. They're going to kill rats at the *ville* before the Yule feast. On their way here they found a baby on the heath."

I stepped forward and pulled the corner of the blanket away from the baby so they could get a good look at his scrunched up, disgruntled little face. Recognizing his cue, he squirmed uncomfortably and let out a squall that filled the house.

The woman began to weep, and her husband sank to the platform beside her and put his arms around her, and she turned her face into him and cried silently. I thought we were as good as rid of the foundling, but then the husband reached down and lifted the fleece off his wife to reveal their baby, dead in her arms.

"What is it you want from us?" he asked. "Here's our own child. Dead."

Eldlyn knelt down in front of them. "This child is the son of the prefect and his slave Eithne," he said. "The prefect exposed him on the heath, but I don't think it was an accident these two men found him. I think it was God's will, so they could bring him to you to comfort you in your loss. I think God wants you to raise the child as your own."

"What have we done that God wants us all dead? If the prefect exposed him, he doesn't want him alive, and if we take him, what stops the prefect from killing us?"

"I don't think you need to worry about the prefect," Banta said.

"And what do you know of it? I may be a free man, but he's the prefect of a royal *ville*, and this is a royal village. The burial place of a king. The prefect does as he likes here, and no one can say no to him."

"We celebrate the birth of Christ in three weeks," the *masse-thegn* said. "He was born in a stable, and when I saw this baby, he was in a stable. Surely you can see that's a sign from God."

The man had no answer to that reasoning, hemmed in by his faith in God and his belief that divine intervention in the affairs of men could happen at any time. The superstitious weight of the season was too heavy to cast aside. I watched as all the resonances of Christian and pagan belief converged on him, obscuring common sense. The solstice was coming in two weeks, the celebration of the birth of Christ a week later, and the Childermas observation that commemorated Herod's slaughter of the innocent male children in Bethlehem would follow three days after that. The symbolic importance of all those memorials of birth and death and regeneration were more than they could resist. He looked at his wife, and she nodded.

The man took his dead son from his wife's arms and carried him into the shadows at the far end of the room, and I stepped forward and handed the crying baby to her. She accepted the baby and began to unwrap the blanket. When he was unwrapped, she opened the top of her dress, which was stained with the birthing blood of her dead baby, and held him to her warm naked flesh. He opened his mouth, and his hand and lips found her engorged nipple, and he began sucking milk from her breast. That was that. Banta looked at me and smiled. Our problems got farther away with every suck and swallow.

Behind me I heard the thud of something heavy hitting the floor. I turned around and saw the man swinging a pick over his head to break up the hard-packed dirt. His son's stillbirth was a private domestic tragedy and the burial would be private and domestic. Adults who lead public lives as members of a kindred and wider village society are buried in cemeteries and churchyards, public places where their lives can be publically acknowledged and their memories publically preserved, but a dead newborn, while a loss to the kindred and the village, is primarily a loss to the family, and it's always buried in the only place it ever knew or was known, the home where it was born.

This custom would allow the burial to remain a secret, and the substitution of the living baby for the dead one would never be known by anyone not standing in the house right now. Similarly, the prefect would expect the body of an exposed baby to be carried away and the remains scattered by wild animals. He wouldn't bother to look for evidence of his bastard's death, and he wouldn't expect to find evidence of its survival.

Banta and I walked over to where the man was digging, and Banta took the pick from his hands.

"Go see your new son," Banta told him, positioning himself to swing the pick into the hard earth.

He looked at the body of his infant son, wrapped in a bloody birthing cloth, and went to his wife. The *masse-thegn* was praying and watching her nurse the baby. I picked up a shovel and cleared the loose dirt out of the grave into a pile beside the hole. The *masse-thegn* hadn't told us the names of the dead baby's parents, but given my monastic training, like a superstition I couldn't shake, I was thinking of them as Joseph and Mary.

We slept in the stable that night. Eldlyn made certain that we had enough wood to keep the fire blazing high and warm the room. The horse couldn't believe its luck. In the middle of the morning the *masse-thegn* came to take us to the *ville*. It had stopped snowing before dawn, and we could hear the voices of the villagers celebrating the new birth drifting to us clearly in the cold air.

"They said to thank you again," Eldlyn said. "She sewed the likeness of king Aldfrith onto the baby's blanket. That's what they're naming him."

"That's them sorted," Banta said. "Now we've got work to do."

Eldlyn helped us load our ratcatching gear into the cart and hitch the horse. The horse was reluctant to leave the warmth of the stable, but since he was a horse his feelings on the matter were of no concern to us. It took us almost an hour to get to the *ville* through the unbroken snow; our tracks were the only blemish on the glittering white surface of the land.

The royal *ville* was on high ground on the other side of a frozen brook off to the left of the road, secure behind a stone wall topped by a wooden palisade. If Eldlyn hadn't been with us we'd never have found the turnoff in the snow. The *ville* wasn't the largest one we'd ever ratted, nor the smallest, either. A modest hall by royal standards, fifteen or twenty meters long and ten wide, a scattering of smaller houses for the occupants, sunken thatched roof houses for the *ceorls* and *theows* that looked like great mounds of snow.

Men were shoveling paths from the houses to the hall and the other buildings. There was a stone chapel and a large stable and a *feorm* barn. The *ville* might not be much visited these days, but in the past it had been frequented often enough by the king and his *gesith* to need an infrastructure that would accommodate and protect them. I reckoned thirty or forty people were living there, ready to serve the king if he ever showed up. At the moment they were preparing for the Yule festivities and the Christmas celebration.

"How long will it take you to kill the rats?" the *masse-thegn* asked while we waited at the gate for the *tún-geréfa*.

"It's hard to say," Banta said. "Rats are going to be in their holes trying to stay warm, same as everyone. We'll have to send the ferrets in to drive them out so the dogs can get them. Lots of their bolt holes will be covered with snow, and we won't know where they are to block them."

The *tún-geréfa* arrived at the gate in the middle of Banta's lament about how difficult it was going to be to kill rats in this weather. He looked us over and smiled. "Nice horse."

"These men are ratcatchers come to rat the *ville* before the Yule celebrations," the *masse-thegn* said. "They were delayed by the storm and spent the night in the village."

"No one told me about ratcatchers," the *geréfa* frowned.

We just stood there, letting our cart full of ferrets and dogs and rat catching gear do our talking for us. Here and there the sun shone through the thinning clouds, producing discrete, blinding spots of pure white on the snowy fields around us. The *geréfa* squinted in our direction and finally nodded, motioning us inside.

"Have you added ratcatching to your usual duties?" he asked Eldlyn when the *masse-thegn* followed us through the gate.

"I haven't visited in a week," he said. "I'm here to offer the sacraments."

"There's one or two as could use the sacraments," the *geréfa* acknowledged.

The hall was built on the highest ground inside the wall. It was set back on a plateau that contained the hall and kitchen and bakery, and its situation had the effect of making it seem to grow in size as you got closer and more of it came into view. It was a subtle, clever bit of site exploitation that enhanced the importance of the hall as you approached, increasing the stature of its owner—the perfect building for a royal ego.

The *geréfa* lifted the latch of the heavy door, and the way he had to lean into it demonstrated its mass and the resistance of its inertia. Royal *ville*s in Northumbria are robustly constructed because a king never knows when a heavily armed *hird* from a rival kindred might show up to drag him out of his country estate and hang him from the nearest tree. They're as defensible as they are comfortable and well-situated.

The interior of the hall was lit only by the fire in the hearth and what bluish winter light came through the window openings in the end walls. The tall thatched roof was supported by a network of heavy beams. I turned a professional eye toward the sooty underside of the thatch. Your black rats are climbers and prefer to live high up out of the reach of most of the things that eat them, while your brown rats are diggers. Wooden buildings with thatched roofs are more likely to have black rats, so the first thing you do is look up; in stone buildings with shingle roofs, like churches and monastic buildings, the first thing you do is examine the foundations.

The prefect was having a late breakfast. He was a young buck, just entering his prime, maybe twenty-five winters old. Judging from the look of his clothing, he'd already been up and at it for hours. We'd been told that he was one of those working prefects, a hands-on supervisor and as much an active manager as his *geréfa*. Frequently the prefect of a royal *ville* or hunting *tún* is a member of the king's kindred, or a well-connected appointee who's more interested in having the position than doing the work the position requires, and who delegates everything that means getting dirty and raising a sweat to his *geréfa*, but this prefect was a go-getter marked for advancement in the kindred, which sort sometimes attracts the attention of the wrong people, which is what had happened, and so we'd been called in.

The prefect was picking a roasted duck apart with his fingers, and the bones of the half that he'd already eaten were piled on the boards beside a basket that held a freshly broken loaf. He looked up as we got closer and wiped his hands on a cloth and drank from a wooden cup. The *geréfa* stopped in front of him and introduced Banta and me with a cursory wave.

"Couple of ratcatchers," he said. "Come to rat the *ville* before Yule."

"We were in Eoforwic working at the royal residence, and one of the *cuppe-thegnan* said we might find work here before Yule."

"Is the king making a visit?"

"He just said the king didn't like rats, and we might find work here."

The prefect sat back, turning over the implications of a recommendation by a royal butler that we come here and kill rats and drawing the only conclusion that made sense: a surprise royal visit for Yule. Eoforwic was only thirty miles to the west on Roman pavement. That meant there was a lot of work to do in a short time. He drained his cup and stood up.

"See that the servants clean the royal chamber top to bottom," he told his *geréfa*. "Fresh linen, change the hangings, and lay a fire in the hearth. I want that fire burning night and day so the heat works into the walls and roof. I want the chamber so warm the king has to walk around bare-assed."

Then he turned his attention to Banta and me. "You two come with me. I'll show you the barns and stables."

He stepped around the table, and we turned to leave and saw that a woman had been strung up against one of the massive posts that supported the loft beams. She was younger than the prefect, not yet twenty winters was my guess, with the ginger hair of a Dál Riata Pict, probably captured in a Northumbrian raid and sold south. Her wrists were bound, and the other end of the rough hemp rope was looped over a horizontal timber. She'd been pulled up so that only the balls of her feet supported her weight. The tattered back of her linen dress was striped with dried blood; she'd been beaten hard enough with a thin stick to raise bloody welts across her shoulders and spine.

Eldlyn came up short. "*Jesu Christi*," he said.

"Sorry you had to see this," the prefect said. "I know she embroiders for you and you've some affection for her, but she stole a penny from the account box, and I had to punish her. I could have cut off her hand, but I've a soft spot for her myself, so I let her off with a beating instead. Why ruin a good slave?"

Banta set his jaw, and his eyes moved over the blood-stiffened cloth that covered the woman's back. I knew that despite his reluctance to become attached to things and even in spite of his anxiety that we'd stumbled onto an elvish changeling, he'd taken a shine to the little tyke, and he wasn't best pleased to see how the prefect had treated his mother.

The *masse-thegn* stepped over to the woman and brushed the hair away from her face. Her head was lolling to the side, and she was only semi-conscious. "How long has she been hanging here?"

"Since last evening when my wife discovered the theft. She had her baby yesterday morning, and when my wife told her to get it ready to take to the heath she wailed and fought, and I had to hit her a few times to make her mind. It wasn't until I got back that Eogiva discovered the theft. Eithne admitted she'd put the penny in the swaddles for whoever found the baby. I beat her and left her there all night as a warning. Can't condone thievery. And now I have to go back and try to find the penny. That's what comes of marrying a thrifty woman: a fool's errand with snow everywhere. How are the roads? It was getting bad on the ride home yesterday."

"Snow up to your knees and higher," Banta said. "Maybe drifts in some places."

"Focking inconvenience," the prefect muttered. "Come on, let's go to the stable. How long will it take to kill the rats?"

He started for the door of the hall, but Eldlyn, standing beside the beaten, exhausted Eithne, detained him again. "How long will you keep her here?"

The prefect hesitated and looked at the priest. "Punishment's a full day. I'll take her down tonight after the evening meal."

He turned away from Eldlyn, and we left the hall.

Outside it was uncomfortably bright after the interior of the hall, and we stood in the shoveled area of the threshold yard until our eyes adjusted.

"Priests are squeamish about handing out punishment," the prefect said. "But they hand out penances like they're paid a Mercian shilling for every prayer they make you say. Still, I reckon I deserved this. I took her to the hay loft and got her with child, and then she started to get ideas above her station. Wanted me to free her. Can you reckon it?" He shook his head in disbelief. "Free a perfectly healthy breeding slave. Uppity focking Picts."

"Priests don't have to run a royal *ville*," Banta said.

"Just so," the prefect agreed. "Been a ratcatcher all your life?"

"Learned my craft from my father."

"How long will it take?" he asked again, remembering what he'd been asking when the priest interrupted him earlier.

"Can't say until you show me where they are."

The prefect nodded and started across the open area between the hall and the big stable. We followed him. Before we set out on the journey to Driffield, Brorda told us everything about the prefect that was in his file. He was a member of Æthelred's kindred, a distant cousin, apparently, and the son of a woman who'd been married into another kindred to make an alliance. He was remote enough from Catræth to be overlooked in the purge that followed Æthelred's exile, in fact, he hadn't even been old enough to carry iron then, but he hadn't been forgotten by Sicga, the kinsman who'd arranged to have Æthelred exiled instead of killed, or by Osbald, who'd inherited the leadership of the kindred after Sicga took himself to Lindisfarne to become a monk.

The plan was for Æthelred to leave Aachen while Big Karl was off completing his annexation of lower Saxony—dedicating a church here, killing a few hundred hostages there—and slip unobserved across the Frisian sea. He was supposed to come ashore on a stretch of deserted beach under the crumbling cliffs about ten miles east of the royal *ville* and then cross the *weald* to Driffield, where his distant cousin was the prefect. He'd hide there all winter and in the spring, probably at Easter, when the Northumbrians liked to stage their revolutions because of the symbolism, his kindred would rise up and kill the king and restore Æthelred to the throne in Eoforwic.

It was a good plan, but it was premature. Æthelred was getting impatient after twelve winters of banishment in Aachen, but it turns out that twelve winters wasn't long enough for everyone in Northumbria to forget why they'd deposed him in the first place, and the details of the plan leaked into the wrong ears, ears that belonged to one of Brorda's whores, put in position and told to keep her legs and her ears open for just such an intelligence gathering opportunity.

Brorda couldn't kill Æthelred while he was under Big Karl's protection, but he could interfere with his schemes in Northumbria. If the distant cousin was removed from his position as prefect of the remote royal *ville* and replaced by someone from outside of Æthelred's kindred, that clandestine hideout would be denied him, and his plan to return postponed for at least another winter. Offa had made a stabilizing accommodation with king Ælfwald that was keeping Mercia's northern border peaceful enough so that he could turn his attention west to the *Bret-wilisc* on the other side of the dyke. He didn't need Æthelred back on the throne creating destabilizing unrest in Northumbria.

We followed the prefect into the stable, walking on either side of him and a half step behind. I closed the door behind us.

"The grain barrels stay in the granary unless the king and the *gesith* come. Then we move them in here. Hay and straw in the loft year round."

The prefect gestured up at the sheaves piled under the rafters in the hay loft. The stable was big enough to house fifty horses in two wings that extended north and south from the two story central structure. At the moment only two of the stalls were occupied. There was a large wooden water trough in the center of an open space just inside the small entrance door. There was a small farrier's forge and an iron anvil and a work bench against the wall to the left side of the double stable doors. The water in the trough was iced over, and there was a patch of ice on the dirt floor beside it where some had been spilled in the filling. As soon as we saw the inside of the stable the choreography of the killing ground was clear to both of us without having to confer.

The prefect started forward again, and we followed him. "The stalls are mucked and ready. We'll fork fresh straw into them when the king arrives, but all the bedding and fodder are in the loft until then. That's where the rats live." He pointed up as he walked beside the frozen trough and stepped onto the ice.

I swept his feet out from under him with a hard kick as they touched the ice, and his legs flew forward, and he flung his arms out to the sides in an involuntary attempt to regain his balance. Banta grabbed his left arm, and I grabbed his right arm, and we lifted and turned his body as it hung there for the longest fraction of a second the prefect had ever lived. As he began to fall we guided him backward, and Banta put his free hand on his chest to accelerate his momentum. We dropped to the ground with the prefect between us, driving the back of his neck onto the edge of the trough, breaking it with a loud crack.

The prefect's body slid down against the side of the trough, his head twisted forward, resting sickeningly on his chest, attached to his distended, broken neck by muscle and tendon but not his spine. He twitched once and shat himself, and his eyelids fluttered, and his dying sigh drifted up toward the rats hiding in the lofty. The murder had only taken us three or four seconds to accomplish.

"Focking ice is dangerous," Banta said, getting to his feet.

I rolled away from the prefect and stood up.

"I reckon I better run to the hall and tell them the prefect had an accident," I said. "Lucky there's a *masse-thegn* here to give him the sacrament."

"You know," Banta said, brushing off the knees of his trousers, "most of the time you do your duty because you have to. Brorda gives you an order, and you make it happen. But every once in a while it's a focking pleasure."

he Swift Flight of a Sparrow

The length of man's life on earth, compared to the time before and after, is like the swift flight of a sparrow through a winter mead hall, when you're eating supper with your companions. The fire warms the hall, but outside winter storms rage, and the sparrow flies in one door and out another. After a short space of fair weather, it's gone, flying from winter into winter. Man lives his life in the blink of an eye, but we know nothing of what follows or what went before.

Ecclesiastical History of England
—Bede

Godmundingaham
Winterfylleth, 790

It was the seventh anniversary of my wife's death, the first day of winter, and I was in the church in Godmundingaham. My presence there wasn't an expression of devout faith, because my only devotion now was to Oswith's memory, and my faith was buried with her in Elmet. It was just a place to go out of the depressing rain where I could be alone with my thoughts and feel sorry for myself. If I'd had anything to drink, it would have been an ideal way to spend the afternoon.

I'd been in Eoforwic, stopping briefly with my friend Sprot and his family, his wife and three small children, the middle boy named after me, when the message from Brorda arrived, and now I was about two-thirds of the way to Beoferléa. Last night I'd stayed in a village called Thorntún, in the house of the *masse-thegn* who kept the small church, dedicated to St. Michael—more a chapel, really—a wooden building with a wooden cross in front, anchored in a rock cairn.

The *masse-thegn* had dreams of one day having a stone church with a stone cross outside, but, after the last few years of bad harvests and sporadic diseases, the countryside around Thorntún was so sparsely populated that I didn't see it happening in his lifetime. He was one of Brorda's housekeepers in Northumbria, maintaining an out-of-the-way safe house sanctuary for Mercian agents operating in the southern part of Northumbria, which had formerly been the independent kingdom of Diera. He provided a meal, a blanket by the fire, and the sacraments, and he used the small stipend he got from Tamoworthig to feed the poor.

Brorda had something he wanted me to take care of in Beoferléa, a town that had grown up around the minster founded by John of Beoferléa, a former Archbishop of Eoforwic. John of Beoferléa had been trained by Hild in Streanshalch and gone on to bigger things, and at the end of his life he'd returned to the minster he founded, died, and was buried there. A common and undramatic career arc for a successful bishop who was more of a competent administrator than a charismatic, badger-whispering crazy man of the sort the Church liked to canonize. Brorda wanted me to locate and copy some bit of documentation in their library without their knowledge—a routine exercise in intelligence gathering, the sort of errand that had no great urgency, so I had time for a side trip to Godmundingaham.

I'd made the detour to Godmundingaham while on the tramp from Eoforwic because I'd never been there. It was the place that figured in the conversion story that Bede had included in his *History*—the location of the pagan idols that the high priest Coifi had thrown down while in the grip of a zealous frenzy immediately following his realization that Christ was the Way, the Truth, and the Life, as well as the only option if Coifi wanted to keep his head and his cushy job.

Like many stories almost two centuries old, I suppose there's *some* truth to it; I'd come to see the place, to walk on the dirt of the old pagan holy site, hoping, maybe, to feel some residual power of the old gods, hoping, maybe, to feel closer to Oswith for an hour or two. I'd been tramping around the kingdoms for six years, and I'd seen hundreds of the old pagan sanctuaries—stone circles on isolated heaths, sacred wells and springs in the deep forest, solitary monoliths on desolate stretches of moorland— but they were as empty of divine grace and pre- ternatural energy as every church I'd been in since Oswith had died.

The cluster of houses that made up the vil- lage of Godmundingaham was twenty rods downslope from the stone church, which I as- sumed had been erected on the old pagan holy place, because that's what the Church liked to do. When generations of people had gone to an oak grove sacred to Wōden, Tīw, and Þunor to worship their wooden effigies, hang sacrificial offerings in the branches of the trees, and bask in their terrible presence, it only made sense that the Church would cut down the oak trees to symbolically eradicate the influence of the old gods and use that timber to build a wooden church dedicated to the nailed god. As a transi- tional ploy, it had worked for centuries to calm any lingering nostalgia for the old ways, and, as generations passed, the ache faded from living memory and became folklore—the stories your granny tells around the fire on a winter night.

The church and graveyard occupied the crest of the low hill, the graves of the dead who wanted to advertise their devotion to the nailed god marked with wooden crosses, and the graves of the more traditionally-minded marked with rune stones. The house that be- longed to the *masse-thegn* was close by, to the south. One hundred and sixty winters had come and gone since Northumbria's conversion, and though the original wooden church had been replaced by a stone building, the timbers that supported the roof used to be trees in that oak grove dedicated to Þunor, Wōden, and Tīw, and I looked up at them and imagined pendent sacrifices swaying in the breeze over pools of blood—horses, sheep, goats, men.

Like most churches, this one was aligned east to west, with the altar on the eastern end of the rectangular nave under a window that would admit the dawn light on Easter Sunday to blind the faithful. The altar was a massive wooden table, a hand's length in thickness, probably a diagonal slice of one of the oldest oaks in the original grove, and had been polished and carved with Christian symbols along the edges. There was a low, stone baptismal font close to the altar. The church must have a patron, because the opposing round windows, high up in the east and west walls, were glazed.

I allowed myself a little smile at the thought that if a sparrow flying by on a stormy night was tempted by the light from the interior of the church and tried to seek shelter inside, it was in for a lethal surprise; better to fly through the unglazed window of the local mead hall, where the air was apt to be smoky and the noise raucous but the hope of shelter from the storm wouldn't be obliterated by a sudden impact with an invisible barrier.

My dead wife came to me in dreams less and less over the years. I didn't blame her; my life must have become something of a disappointment to her. I know it had to me. No matter what service I performed, I was unable to escape my indenture to the Mercians. As long as Brorda and Offa were in power, I would be their *sundornotu geréfa* in the north, spying and killing at their pleasure. I knew Oswith still visited the children in their dreams, and the thought made me happy; the children needed her advice more than I did because they were in a position to follow it, and I was not.

I was alone in the church, wrapped in my cloak. I'd circled the village and approached across the stubble of the harvested furlongs and through the intermittent woods to the north, so no one had marked my coming; I intended to sit quietly and think about Oswith, to commemorate the day of her death in silent contemplation of loss and the transitory nature of life, and I couldn't think of a more appropriate place to do it than the empty church in Godmundingaham.

With any luck I'd fall asleep in the silence, and Oswith would visit me, and we could talk as we used to do when she was alive. I could ask after the children and find out the latest news— whether Mæthild, who was fourteen now, had turned her analytical attention to boys yet, as serious in her evaluation of their potential as husbands and fathers as she was in everything else; if Torhtmund, a winter younger, and at the age when playing at the shield wall was really practicing for the shield wall, was starting to think about getting his iron in a couple of winters. My younger daughter Osgiva was the emotional heart of our family, sensitive and considerate, offering support where Mæthild was inclined to offer guidance or direction, or possibly disapproval; was she starting to think about a religious life, as she'd once mentioned? I hoped not. Gulhere, the youngest at eleven winters, idolized his cousin Ordgar, who had attached himself to my children as their protector and friend and surrogate brother. Ordgar was a *geréfa* now, working for Creda. Was Gulhere thinking of following his cousin in service to the *ealdorman*?

If I dreamed of Oswith, there was a good chance she'd tell me how they all were, and I could tell her that I was well, and she could pass that information on to the children. If they cared, after six winters, whether I was well or not. I saw them two or three times from Yule to Yule. Not often enough, in the winters of their fading childhood and gathering adulthood, to make a difference in their lives.

I closed my eyes and thought of her taking care of the children, weaving, sharing a bath with me at the end of the week, making butter, talking to the children, scrubbing the table with a stiff brush, all the random activities I'd witnessed over the winters we'd been together, and I was starting to drift into sleep when the church door wrenched open with a loud scream of hinges and startled me awake.

The *masse-thegn* stumbled into the nave leaving wet footprints behind him, propelled forward across the stone floor by some unbalancing force. His toe caught a seam between the pavers, and he sprawled headlong onto his face.

Before I could react, two men followed him into the church. They had their hoods up against the weather, and I could see raindrops beaded up on the nap. One of the men continued after the *masse-thegn*, leaving his own line of wet footprints beside the priest's; the other turned and dropped the wooden bar into the brackets to secure the church door.

"Where is it?" the man who'd followed the *masse-thegn* demanded. He kicked the priest's leg, and the priest rolled to his side and drew his knees toward his chin. He looked like they'd worked him over for quite a while before bringing him to the church—his face was already bruising and there was blood in the stubble on his jaw. His hair and clothing were soaked from the rain, and the paving stones underneath him were pooling with water.

"I told you, there's nothing here," he said. He slurred his denial, spitting out some blood.

The second man walked from the door to the middle of the nave. The priest scrabbled away from him toward the altar, leaving a damp trail like a slug. The church was perhaps three rods on the long sides, a rod and a half on the short. In addition to the two windows in the east and west ends, there were three narrow windows high up in the north and south walls, so while there was faint watery light, there wasn't much because of the rain, and I was in the shadow of the southwest corner, wrapped up in a brown cloak; they hadn't noticed me yet.

The man who'd barred the church door

stepped between me and the *masse-thegn*; his mate, standing on the far side of the body on the floor, kicked the *masse-thegn* hard in the ribs. The priest rolled over on his side with a grimace, his face visible between the ankles of the man standing with his back to me, and that's when the priest saw me sitting in the corner. His eyes widened in surprise and then closed painfully as the man kicked him again in the back. But the one standing with his back to me had seen the priest look in my direction, noticed the momentary surprise that had nothing to do with them beating the shite out of him on the floor of his own church, and turned to see what had caught his attention.

"Oi," he barked as I came into dim focus.

His partner looked up and saw me sitting in the corner and stepped over the *masse-thegn*, who was writhing on the pavers, and stood shoulder to shoulder with his mate. We were separated by about twenty feet, enough distance for me to get to my feet before they could do much more than register my presence. I looped the shoulder strap of my bag over my head and threw my cloak open over my right shoulder, so I could reach behind my back, closing my fingers on the leather-wrapped hilt of my *seax*. We stood there, balanced on the edge of violence, hesitating to make the move that would end in blood.

I could see that they both had knives in their belts, but they weren't reaching for them. We assessed our positions, weighing the odds of winning the fight, or at least limiting our injury. I was closer to the door than they were. Each kick had moved the priest deeper into the nave. I could slide to my left and lift the bar from the iron brackets before they could reach me and then either slip outside and run for it or face them with a stout club if I preferred not to use my iron. The shorter of the two cut his eyes to the door and back to me, and I knew he was thinking along the same lines.

"Who are you, then?" the taller man asked. "Some sheep-wanker wants confession?"

I'd never been in Godmundingaham in my life, and the question made me realize that he must be a stranger to the village too. There couldn't be more than fifty or sixty people in the whole parish, including the nearby farmsteads. Everyone had to know everyone. The closest village was the one that had grown around the big royal *ville* a couple of miles to the west. That place had been a habitation since the Romans had built an outpost there, not far off Humber Street, a Roman branch road that ran south to the river. It had its own church because it had been the location of Edwin's winter palace, the scene of the famous mead hall in Bede's *History*. So who were these men, and why were they roughing up the priest? Back in my former life, when I'd been an assistant advocate in Elmet, I would have been obliged to intervene to stop the assault, but my current life as a *sundornotu geréfa* argued for a more circumspect approach. This was none of my business. For all I knew, the priest deserved a beating. I'd known a few who had, and I'd administered two well-deserved beatings to *masse-thegns* myself. I felt like I was in no position to make a hasty judgment.

"Just a man who came in out of the rain for some quiet prayer," I said.

The shorter of the two glanced at the door again and took a step in that direction. I took two steps to my left, shortening the geometric base of the triangle formed by him and me and the door. He stopped moving.

"Help me," the *masse-thegn* groaned and coughed some more blood; a couple of teeth clicked onto the stone floor.

The taller man turned and kicked the priest in the ribs again, the force of it lifting him off the floor enough that I saw pavement under his robes.

"What's this all about?" I asked.

"Caught him with my sister," the shorter of the two men said.

If that was true, the two men might be within their rights to beat the priest. A man caught in a compromising position with an unmarried woman by her male relatives was liable for a beating, worse if she was a virgin or an adulterous wife: then they could kill him with impunity. However, if the seducer was a priest they were on boggier ground. The priest coughed up still more blood and lay on the stones, breathing hard.

"Then call the *geréfa*," I said. "Appeal him before the *gemót*."

"Nothing will come of that."

206

He was right. Canon law protects church-men from the consequences of their secular crimes. Maybe they were just administering what little rough secular justice the priest was ever going to receive—something more memo-rable and with more deterrent force than a few winters' penance of fasting and prayer. But it bothered me that he thought I was from God-mundingaham, which meant *he* wasn't from Godmundingaham, and if he wasn't from the village, I doubted he caught the priest with his sister. Village priests don't travel all that much, even for clandestine fornication. All their indis-cretions are local.

"He looks like he understands the error of his ways now," I said. "Best find the *geréfa* be-fore you're liable to an appeal for assault."

"You know a lot about it," the taller man said.

I shrugged. "I know what I know."

"What would you do if you found a *masse-thegn* with your sister?"

Before I could answer him the priest lurched to his knees behind them and then, un-able to maintain his balance, fell over again. Things had clearly gone far enough, and I had to do something unless I was prepared to stand there while these two killed the *masse-thegn* in front of his own altar.

"No idea," I said. "But you've done all you're going to do to the *masse-thegn*." I stepped side-ways to the door and slipped the bar from the brackets. They didn't move, and I didn't turn

my back on them. I opened the door and started to back out of the church. Behind me I could
hear rain falling.

"I'm getting the *geréfa*," I told them. "Either
be gone when I get back or appeal him for
whatever he's done."

The taller man's eyes shifted over my
shoulder, and I just had enough time to understand that he was looking at something behind
me when I felt my head explode and everything went black.

The next thing I was aware of was
how much my head hurt. I was face
down on the floor, and my hands were
tied behind me. I kept my eyes closed and tried
to push my awareness through the throbbing
pain, which matched my heartbeat. I could hear
movement behind me, feet shuffling on the
stone floor. I opened my eyes a narrow slit and
found the wall of the church less than a foot
from my nose. Someone had hit me from behind, which meant that there were more than
two men, but I had no idea how many more or
if they were all in the church with me now.

"It's got to be here somewhere," a man said.

"Where? Look around. This is a big empty
stone room. There's no place to hide anything."

I heard them struggling, and the priest
moaning, and his moans cut off in a liquid
splash.

My feet weren't bound. I rolled over slowly
so my back was to the wall. There were two

men in the room, but the shorter man had been replaced by a different shorter man, who now had my *seax* thrust through his belt. They were holding the priest by the shoulders and the back of the neck, forcing his head into the baptismal font. The priest was struggling, but they had him wedged between them, and there wasn't much he could do except to try not to inhale. When his struggles grew weaker they pulled his head back, and he coughed up holy water—which, despite his best efforts, had found its way down his gullet—and desperately gulped in air.

"Where is it?" the man who'd taken my *seax* asked the priest.

My cloak was spread on the stones nearby and the contents of my bag were spilled out on the wool. There was a spare tunic and another pair of socks, my flint and steel and bag of tinder, my ear spoon and tweezers and a little scissors. My leather-working tools were dumped in another little pile—the skiving knife, the half-moon trimmer, the three awls, the iron stamps and rolled leather mallet, and the bronze needles and spool of waxed thread and the heavy leather squares with samples of my tooling and stamping. I looked at the church door; it was barred again. I realized my hands were tied with my own belt. I thought about rolling over there and trying to cut myself loose with the skiving knife, but when I looked back at them, one of the men was looking at me.

"Maybe *he* knows."

"Where is it?" the other one asked.

"What?"

"That's what the *masse-thegn* said." He kicked the priest, breathing heavily on the floor beside the stone baptismal font.

I felt like I was two or three seconds behind what was happening. I had to think for a moment how what they were saying applied to me. This wasn't encouraging because these two didn't strike me as the sort that were capable of the subtle logic or tangled sophism that would leave a minster-trained man like me, an assistant advocate in the *gemót* courts, scratching his head and wondering what the point of a question was.

I closed my eyes tight and listened to the throbbing in my head, and when I opened them again they were both halfway across the nave. Things seemed to be happening in disconnected segments, as if my awareness had become a string of disjointed moments.

They dragged me to my feet, and then one of them hit me in the center of my gut, paralyzing my ability to breathe, producing a suffocating helplessness that radiated away from my gut and settled like a hand on my throat. My knees sagged, and they pulled me across the stones and dropped me beside the priest.

"Where is it?"

"Who is this man?" the priest croaked out. "Why are you doing this?"

"Don't you recognize one of your flock?" the taller man asked. "Doesn't the good shepherd lay down his life for his sheep?"

The priest squinted at me through his

bruised and swollen eyelids, struggling to get me in focus. "I've never seen him in my life," he said.

That seemed to confuse them. I reckon they understood that I had much less value to coerce the priest into telling them whatever they wanted to know if I wasn't from his parish.

"What are you doing here?"

It took me a minute to regain control of my breathing.

"I came in here to pray. I'm going to Beofer-léa to make book covers in their scriptorium."

"Are you a monk, then?"

"Just a leather cutter," I said.

"He don't know shite," the shorter one said. "It's down to the priest."

"I told you," the priest said. "There is no treasure."

It had been a hard year in Northumbria—an abbreviated growing season because of the late spring and early autumn, and then another sparse harvest. Such conditions always sent men away from their homes so that there was more food to increase the chances of survival for those who remained. Men on the road often threw in together for protection or to increase their persuasive force when visiting a *tún* looking for a handout; from there it was a short step to theft and robbery and the brief, miserable life of a wolfshead on marginal subsistence until the *fyrd* tracked you down and killed you.

I assumed these men had struck out on their own rather than stay at home and starve, but something about their speech was curious. Usually the members of an *ad hoc hird* of itinerant ruffians were from different places and their accents were different, but these men shared the distinctive accent of the area around Ghellinges, north of Eoforwic, an area that was a stronghold of Æthelred's kindred.

I began to make some connections. Maybe I was slow, what with being clubbed from behind and the resulting headache, but three men all coming from the territory controlled by Æthelred's kindred started me thinking. Brorda had wanted me to investigate the latest recorded transactions from the local hundred *gemóts*, archived in the Beoferléa scriptorium. He was interested in the flow of coin and goods and land and what could be learned from the shifting currents of Northumbrian legal activity, and, because of my experience in the Elmetsætan judiciary, I was often given missions that involved snooping through the legal records in monastic archives.

Brorda believed that the frequent revolts and usurpations and changes of dynasty that had been the hallmark of Northumbrian polity for the last century were always preceded by a realignment among the *thegns* of the kingworthy kindreds, and that those shifting allegiances were signaled by *gemót* activity, particularly marriages and the ownership of land—legal business that was recorded and housed in local monastic archives.

Offa didn't need trouble in Northumbria. Or rather, he needed a certain *kind* of trouble that was to his advantage. In the past, Northumbrian kings had diverted the mischief of their rivals by starting wars with Mercia, just as Mercian kings had followed the same strategy by starting wars with Northumbria. Chaos in Northumbria had to be controlled—chaos that kept the Northumbrian dynasties at one another's throats, not marching south.

It was also in my personal interest to keep the Northumbrians busy with one another because if they invaded Mercia the most direct route was right through the heart of Elmet, where my family and my kindred lived. In living memory the best way of keeping Northumbria in chaos was just to stay out of their way and let them be chaotic. They were experts.

Northumbria had been roiling with dynastic power struggles since Mercia had eclipsed it as the foremost kingdom of Britain. The latest was between a kindred descended from one of Ida's bastards (represented by former kings Æthelwold Moll and his son Æthelred) and the Leodwaldinga, one of the legitimate lines descended from Ida.

Two winters ago, an *ealdorman* called Sicga had murdered king Ælfwald, who'd been on the throne for nine prosperous winters, to pave the way for Æthelred to return from his exile in the court of Big Karl in Aachen, but Sicga had either overestimated his support among the other kindreds or that support evaporated like morning dew (as such support frequently does); in any case, a cousin of the murdered king had emerged from the post-assassination struggle and taken brief control before Æthelred could get back to Northumbria. In the aftermath of the botched revolt, Sicga had retired to Lindisfarne to contemplate the untoward results of a failed coup attempt, and Æthelred remained in Aachen.

Unfortunately for Osred, the winner of the power struggle, he wasn't as successful or well-liked as his dead cousin, and when the crops failed two harvests running, the people interpreted it as a sign of God's disfavor. When that explanation for empty bellies takes root, rival dynasties begin to get ideas, and at the moment, the kindred in the best position to take advantage of the opportunity those empty bellies presented was Æthelred's.

There was always the danger that Æthelred's kindred would get it right this time; that they would exploit the popular belief that God had deserted the Leodwaldinga, which would make even Æthelred's return seem like a step in the right direction. Once on the throne again, Æthelred could divert domestic attention toward a foreign adventure against Mercia on the promise of recapturing the glory days of the last century, before everything had gone to shite.

And here were some thugs from the home territory of Æthelred's kindred looking for treasure in the south. Revolutions are a costly business—people have to be bribed; soldiers have to be paid; weapons have to be bought—and Æthelred's kindred have always been devout adherents to the prudent financial philosophy of never paying for their revolutions with their own coin. If things go wrong, it's always a good idea to have chests full of silver in reserve to buy your way out of the consequences. That's how Sicga's head had ended up bowed in prayer at Lindisfarne instead of looking down from a spike over the north gate of Eoforwic.

The short man snorted in disgust. "You'd like us to believe that, wouldn't you? No treasure." "This is the place they threw down the pagan idols. It was the biggest pagan temple in Northumbria before they converted. Sure as flies on a dead man's eyes there's treasure here. There's focking *glass* in the windows."

People believe what they want to believe, and these idiots wanted to believe that there was pagan gold hidden in a bare stone room in the middle of nowhere, and they refused to believe the contrary evidence of their eyes because the focking *windows* were glazed.

"Maybe you ought to look under the floor," I said.

What must that sparrow have thought? One minute improbably flying through a blizzard in the dark, when any self-respecting sparrow would be burrowed deep within the sheltering boughs of a pine tree out of the wind, the next inside a mead hall, loud with the celebratory babble of drunken *thegns* feasting at the table in front of the warm hearth fire, and before the sparrow even realized that this might be a good place to stop for the night, safe and warm up there in the rafters, it was out the other door and back into the blizzard.

It was a metaphorical sparrow, I get that, but still it must have been as confused as I was: one minute taking a brief rest on my way from Eoforwic to Beoferléa and the next a captive of three dimwits from Æthelred's kindred. I was a metaphor for the metaphor—like the infinitely regressing images in opposing mirrors, the sparrow and I arced away from one another into infinity.

"What?"

The shorter man, who seemed to be in charge, looked at me as if I'd broken a fundamental rule of being a captive.

"There's no place to hide anything in the altar," I said. "It's a solid slab of wood. And you couldn't hide a handful of coin in the baptismal font even if it was hollow. There's nothing up there under the roof but oak rafters. The only place you could hide anything in here is under the paving stones."

They looked around at the floor of the church. It was paved with stone that looked like it had been looted from some Roman site, a common economy when constructing the fabric of a church. I reckoned the stones had been in the ground for a long time and wouldn't be pried up without a struggle. A close examination of the seams between the stones would give these dolts something to do while I thought of a way out of this mess.

"He's right, Alrys" the taller man said to the shorter man.

The shorter man, now identified helpfully

as Alrys, nodded and his eyes narrowed. "Does this village have a forge?" he asked the priest.

The village was barely large enough for a community cess pit, but I kept my opinions to myself. I'd already strayed close to the edge of acceptable captive behavior, and I didn't want to provoke him further. I had to get my hands free so I could get them around the throat of the man who'd hit me from behind, and I couldn't do that if he decided to beat me.

Alrys kicked the priest. "I'm talking to you."

"No," the priest said.

"There's a common plough barn," the other man said. "There might be something there we can use."

"Go look."

The man who wasn't called Alrys crossed the nave, unbarred the door, and went outside into the rainy afternoon, leaving Alrys to inspect the floor for indications that something was buried underneath it. He started near the door and began working his way toward the altar.

"Who are these idiots?" I whispered.

The priest shook his head. The split, swollen lips and broken teeth they'd given him made it difficult to understand his whispering. "Came this afternoon. Wanted me to show them where the treasure is."

"Is there treasure?"

"No." He looked at me as if I were as stupid as the thugs.

Every pagan mound, barrow, and stone circle was rumored to be the site of buried treasure, and many had been dug up by robbers desperate enough to risk the accompanying curses, because what good is a rumored hoard if it isn't protected by a rumored curse against anyone who disturbs it? The spirits of the dead are famously possessive of their undiscovered troves.

"Where are the *folc*?"

"*Brycgweorc*," he said.

"Don't they have work here?"

"Harvest's in."

"Any chance someone will come?"

"No."

It was up to me then.

"Can you untie my wrists?" I rolled over so my back was to the priest.

"Shut it over there," Alrys called out. He was on his hands and knees examining the seams in the floor pavement.

"No," the *masse-thegn* whimpered.

I tested the leather strapping. There was no hope of me loosening it without his help; it was so tight I couldn't feel my fingers. I thought about rushing the man while he was on his hands and knees and kicking his head off his shoulders, but he was facing me. By the time I got to my feet and crossed the space between us, I'd be running into the point of my own *se-ax*.

It's funny how you never truly understand your lot until it changes for the worse. I'd thought that the miserable state of affairs that had become my life couldn't deteriorate much more after Oswith died and I was conscripted by the Mercians and separated from my kindred; now, like that sparrow, I was almost out of the mead hall into whatever comes next.

The church door opened and two men came in carrying an assortment of items from the plough barn—a chipped and rusted coulter, a long-handled reaping hook, a mattock, and a wooden spade. They tracked mud onto the pavers and dripped water.

"Raining harder," one of them said, shaking the water off his hood.

There were three men in the church now, and I wondered how many more were waiting outside.

They dropped the tools, and one of them walked over to us while the other started looking at the seams of the stone pavement.

"You could make this easy and just tell us where it is," the man said when he was standing over the priest.

The priest didn't bother answering. Maybe he was experimenting, varying his responses to see which one didn't earn him a kick. Denying there was treasure hidden in the empty church didn't seem to be working. Silence didn't work either; the man stomped on the priest's left hand, and I heard the crunch of breaking bones. The priest cradled his left hand to his chest with his right hand and sobbed.

"I think we should look in the *masse-thegn*'s house again."

"We already tore it apart," Alrys said. "It's got to be here."

The third man was excavating a seam between paving stones with his knife and had made enough room to slide the point of the reaping hook between the stones. In the absence of anything like a fulcrum, he started working it side to side to exploit the little progress he'd made.

"Need something to brace it on," he said after a moment.

"Anything in the stable? A small keg or a box—something?"

"I'll go look," the man said.

"See if there's a rope and pulley," I said.

The three thugs stopped what they were doing and looked at me again. None of this had anything to do with me, and suddenly I was doing all the thinking for them. Someone had to; it was clear they hadn't thought this through for themselves, and if they gave it up as a bad job the only thing left for them to do was kill us—I needed to keep them busy.

"Those stones are big, and they look like they've been set for a long time. You can throw a rope over the rafters and lift them out with a pulley. Save a lot of work."

"Why would you help us?"

"The sooner you find whatever you're looking for, the sooner you're gone," I said. It sounded like the desperate reasoning of a frightened man, and they were prepared to accept it as such, but I reckoned they'd kill us either way. It made no sense to let witnesses to their many felonies live. Assault on a *massethegn*, assault on me, desecration of a church, theft (if they managed to find anything worth stealing), breaking the *frith* and *mund* of the

Church—what did it matter if they added a couple of murders to the list, especially if that increased their chances of getting away with the rest of it?

"He's right, Leoric" Alrys said.

Leoric nodded and went to the stable to find something to use as a fulcrum and to see if there was a pulley. The longer I kept them busy, the longer I stayed alive, and the more time I had to think of some way to escape them.

Alrys came over and sat on the edge of the baptismal font. "How does a leather cutter know about pulleys?" he said.

I could have talked all day about pulleys thanks to a Geometry teacher in the minster who'd liked to read long passages from Hero of Alexandria's book on moving heavy weights, but I just said, "Saw one on the wharf in Eoforwic once." That seemed to satisfy Alrys, and he looked over at the man who was still digging at the seam between two of the stones.

"Egwahl."

The third man looked up.

"Go see if there's anything to drink in the *masse-thegn*'s house."

Egwahl got to his feet and left the church. It was clear now that Alrys was in charge of the party, and that getting rid of him had to be my first priority. The other two would hesitate if Alrys went down, and a moment's hesitation could mean the difference between me walking out of Godmundingaham or spending eternity in an unmarked grave in the churchyard.

"Thirsty work, prying up a stone floor," I said.

"What would you know about it?"

I shrugged.

"Something about you ain't quite right," Alrys said. He stood up, and I braced myself to be kicked. That seemed to be his preferred mode of interrogation. But before he could put the boot to me, Leoric came back into the church carrying a block of wood; he had a big coil of hemp over one shoulder with a pulley tangled in it. It was a lot of rope; I reckoned maybe a hundred feet. He dropped the wooden block and shrugged out of the coil.

Alrys walked over to examine the rope, and I looked at the priest. He was in bad shape. There comes a time in a beating when even though they stop kicking you, you're too damaged to do anything but lie there; the priest was past that point, and the head thug, Alrys, had decided that there was something not quite right about me, keen judge of character that he was.

They slipped the curved outer edge of the reaping hook into the crack in the pavement and positioned the long wooden shaft over the block and started levering the stone out of the floor. There was a brief screech of iron on stone and then the edge of the paver popped out of the floor. Alrys stood back as Egwahl got on one knee and pulled the stone out of the hole. The three of them crowded around for a look, as if they were expecting a pot of gold to be glittering back at them. Judging from the disappointed slump of their shoulders, there was nothing there but dirt.

I looked around the church. There must have been more than five hundred stones of varying size paving the floor. "That's one," I said.

"Think you're focking funny, do you?"

Alrys walked over, and I braced for a kick, but he surprised me by pulling me to my feet.

"Why should we do all the work when you're a good strong man?"

He stepped behind me, and I could feel him working on the knotted belt, then my hands were free; I had no sensation in them—there were deep red grooves in my wrists the width of my belt—and I began to rub my hands together to bring the blood back.

"Get over there and start pulling up stones," he said, pushing me toward the hole in the floor.

I walked over to the displaced paver and tried to lift up the coulter to set it under the edge of a neighboring paver, but I couldn't grip it tightly, and it slipped out of my numb grasp and fell to the floor with a clang.

"Be a minute before I can hold anything," I said, rapidly clenching and unclenching my fingers into fists.

Alrys walked to the opposite side of the paver that they'd levered out of the floor and pushed it aside with his boot. Then he moved the wooden block into position, picked up the reaping hook, and slipped the back edge of the curved blade under another paver. He applied his weight to the shaft of the reaping hook and there was a little movement, but the stone stayed in the hole.

"Get it out of there," he said to Egwahl.

Egwahl dropped to one knee and slipped the coulter under the stone and jiggled it for a moment, and then slid the stone to the side and looked into the hole, apparently finding more dirt than treasure, because he shook his head in disappointment and stood up again.

"This could take us all night," he said.

"You," Alrys barked at me. "Get to work." He drew my *seax* and stepped to the side as Egwahl handed me the coulter. It was about two feet long. I could force its chipped point under the edge of an in-place paver and lay it across the wooden block and stand on the free end to use my weight to lift the stones. I could also crush his head with it, and that was the application Alrys was worried about.

"Leoric, get to work with the reaping hook."

Leoric picked up the wooden shaft of the hook and started to pry up one of the other pavers. Egwahl crouched down, and when the stones came out of the floor he pushed them aside and looked into the hole. After five minutes there was a small pile of paving stones to one side of a widening unpaved area of the floor.

"How many times do you want to move these stones?" I asked.

"What's that mean?" Alrys looked at the stones and then at me.

"If you want to look under the pavement the

stones are piled on, you have to move them again; the bigger the pile, the more work to move it."

The three thugs paused to consider this basic truth of working with blocks of stone. I was sure that the Romans had some protocol for this kind of work, refined over centuries of monumental civic engineering, but these three weren't Roman engineers. The light was getting dimmer in the church as the late afternoon moved into early evening.

"You're a bright boy," Alrys said. "What do you reckon?"

"Set them against the wall," I said. "Nothing's buried beside the foundations. If there's anything here it will be in the middle of the church."

Leoric and Egwahl took a breath and thought about moving all that stone for the second time, because they rightly understood that they'd be the ones doing the heavy lifting. That was good. I wanted them tired out. I picked up the coulter and slid it under another paver.

"Best get started," Alrys said. "The longer you wait the more stone you have to shift."

They started moving the paving stones against the wall, and I went back to work, but I kept my eye on Alrys and hoped he'd become inattentive. The area of the floor without pavement was now a ragged oval about four by seven feet. The dirt underneath it was compact and firm, and had been channeled here and there by the movement of worms just under the stones, their winding galleries meandering briefly before they disappeared underground again.

Leoric and Egwahl worked fast, and in ten minutes they had the stones arranged along the south wall of the church in three courses. When all the loose pavement had been shifted, the two men picked up the mattock and spade and started digging up the dirt. This was going to leave them with the same problem that displacing the pavers had caused, but I decided to let them work that out for themselves.

The priest had been quiet for some time, an unconscious heap of blood and bruises and broken ribs beside the altar. Alrys hadn't even bothered to kick him for a while.

After half an hour I had quite a large area cleared of stone. All the pavers had been a couple of inches thick and more or less rectangular, having been repurposed as floor covering for the church from the floor of some other building. Then I discovered a stone that must have been a threshold stone because it was three times the length of the others and three times the thickness. It would take a lot more effort to lift it out of the ground. My head throbbed, and I was sweating now, and the light had almost entirely drained from the glazed windows. Leoric had gone back to the priest's house for something to drink and returned with tallow candles that he lit and placed on the pile of paving stones against the south wall and

on the floor beside the excavation, so we had
light to work by. He'd tracked in more water,
and the dirt in the hole had turned into slippery
mud; water was pooled here and there where
they walked.

"This is where the pulley will help," I said.

Leoric and Egwahl came over and looked at
the big stone. They were muddy from digging,
but they weren't excavating to any depth because the ground was hard and their tools were
inadequate, and I reckoned their optimistic ex-
pectation had been that the treasure would only
be a couple of inches down. They started digging along one edge of the paver while I removed the paving stones on either end so we
had room to work. They found the bottom
edge of the stone and started to pry it loose.
They'd hardly begun when the long wooden
shaft of the reaping hook snapped just back of
the tang and dropped Egwahl onto his arse in
the mud.

"Focking hell," he snarled, throwing the broken shaft against the opposite wall of the
church.

Leoric got on his knees to pull the long iron
blade out from under the stone and suddenly
froze. "There's something down here," he said.

"What is it?" Alrys asked.

Leoric gripped the blade of the reaping
hook in both hands and started stabbing at the
ground beside the stone, scooping out the loose
dirt. After a moment he jerked back and scram-
bled aside. "A focking skull," he said.

It was unexpected, but I didn't think too

much of it. It was a common enough practice to bury a priest under the floor of his church, and in the early days, before the church was made of stone and had a paved floor, it had certainly been made of wood with a dirt or a board floor, and the first couple of priests who'd said mass there might well have been buried inside before it became the custom to plant them outside in the churchyard among the mortal remains of their parishioners.

"What's the matter with you? You've seen plenty of skulls," Alrys said.

"Just surprised me is all," Leoric said, recovering his composure.

Leoric dug around the skull and scraped the dirt to the side, and then he slipped both hands into the hole and lifted it clear. Dirt clung to the left side of the skull and packed the empty eye socket. Leoric brushed the dirt off and dug it out of the eye socket with his thumb before he held the skull up for us to admire. Then he set it on the pile of stones, so the dead man could oversee our work.

Leoric got back into place and returned to loosening the dirt along the edge of the stone with the reaping hook blade, but despite cleaning the skull, a bit of bluster that I thought was meant to show us he wasn't afraid, his enthusiasm seemed to have dampened a bit, as if finding a skull in the dirt under a darkened church that used to be a pagan sacrificial grove had awakened old superstitions. I wondered if he was thinking about the curse for disturbing the hoard, even though no one had mentioned one.

After another couple of minutes, he stopped again and reached into the hole with a big smile that seemed to dispel any apprehension and withdrew his hand and tossed a gold coin onto the pavement at Alrys' feet.

"No treasure, eh?" Alrys laughed, and turned to give the unconscious priest a celebratory kick.

I didn't know what to make of that. It seemed impossible that these dolts had actually discovered treasure on the old pagan site, but the evidence of the gold coin was right there on the floor. Still, men lost coins all the time; it could be a coincidence, even though he'd found it under a skull. Although Christians weren't as prone to send a dead man into the ground with grave goods to make things easier for him in the next life, they sometimes buried their dead with items that had been useful or significant in this life; but in general their funeral customs were more thrifty. The priests would tell you that if you lived a virtuous life, everything you needed was waiting for you in heaven, and if you went to the other place, nothing that you could take with you would make it more comfortable.

When we'd removed the paving stones all around the big stone block, I untangled the rope and pulley. The pulley had four wheels, multiplying its lifting capacity by four, and the hemp was as thick as my thumb. I didn't think it would be much trouble to lift the stone clear once the rope was around it. Now that Leoric had made a good beginning, Egwahl joined him and the two set to work with the mattock and spade and soon had improved the narrow, knife-cut trench into a ditch that encircled the stone block, isolating it from the rest of the floor on its pedestal of compressed dirt.

"Here's something," Egwahl said, scraping the spade along the bottom of the ditch. I could tell from the difference in the sound that there was something besides hard-packed dirt down there—maybe a chest. Leoric dropped the mattock and held one of the tallow candles over the hole.

"Focking Christ," he said.

"Stand away," Alrys said and looked into the hole. His face registered discomfort, and he stepped back. The other two stood there uneasily.

"What is it?" I asked.

He gestured for me to have a look. They'd exposed what looked to be a charred section of a log, but it had been carved, and they'd unearthed the rough profile of a grotesque face, the side scraped by the wooden blade of the spade. I reckoned it was one of the original pagan idols.

"It's Þunor," I said.

"How do you know?"

"All right, maybe it's Tīw or Wōden himself, but it's one of them. This was their sacred grove, and when the pagans converted, the chief priest threw down the effigies and built a church."

Alrys cackled with anticipation. "We're a couple of feet away from a hoard of pagan gold," he said.

We worked on one end of the stone and started to lever it up, jamming a couple of smaller pavers under it so I could loop the rope around the width of the stone block two or three times. Then I laid the two pulley blocks out on the floor and started threading the rope through the wheels. I needed three lengths of rope: one to secure the upper pulley block to the roof beams, one to rig between the pulley blocks and lift the weight, and one to secure the lower block to the stone.

I cut the two shorter lengths first, and then I had to thread the long rope through the wheels. A lot of winters separated me from Hero of Alexandria, and I had a couple of false starts, but finally I had it rigged.

"Now what?"

I tied the end of the rope around the broken handle of the reaping hook and threw it over the roof beam above the stone, and then I pulled the line tight and got ready to climb up into the rafters.

"What you think you're doing?"

"We can't just pull it over the beam; it's too heavy and it will break the rope. I have to climb up there and secure the upper pulley block."

"Leoric, you do it."

Leoric spit on his hands and climbed hand over hand to the beam.

"Now what?"

I tossed the pulley blocks up to him. Now I had one of the thugs hanging onto the rafters fifteen feet above us, but there were still two on the floor with me, and Alrys was still holding my *seax*.

"Tie the one block to the beam and let the other one drop out along the length of the rope. Mind you wrap it around the beam two or three times and tie it good and tight," I said.

Egwahl threw the shortest length of rope up to his mate, who bungled the first catch but caught it on the second.

When he had the block secured to the beam, he dropped the other pulley and the wheels squeaked as the rope rolled through them. Fortunately, it didn't bind half way down. When I had the ropes firmly in the wheels I secured the lower block to the rope that was wrapped around the stone and slowly pulled the rigging tight.

"Come back down here," Alrys called up to Leoric, and he slid down the taut line and dropped onto the floor of the church beside us.

"What now?"

"Now you just pull."

"Stand over there," Alrys said, pointing toward the altar.

I stepped over beside the priest.

The three men gripped the rope and heaved, and the stone jerked suddenly up on its end and then off the floor, swinging like a pendulum and spinning around, surprising them with how easy the pulley made it. I could see mud-caked letters carved on the down side: LEG VI. Whatever the stone had been for, it had been carved by a mason in the Sixth Legion. I was familiar with their stone work—it was all over Northumbria.

"It's not that heavy," Egwahl said.

"The pulley makes it light," I said. "One man can probably hold it."

Alrys released his hold on the rope and looked at the other two men. Then Leoric slowly relaxed his grip and stepped away. Egwahl repositioned himself and shifted his footing, but he didn't seem to be straining.

"Help me shift the stone," Alrys said to Leoric, and they guided the swinging stone to one side. Egwahl let out some slack and lowered the stone to the ground beside the hole. Alrys got onto his knees and looked into the hole and scraped some more of the dirt out, but he found that when he wanted to change his position, he was blocked by the stone, sitting on its end beside the hole.

"Lift it out of the way," he said. "I need more room to work."

Egwahl wrapped the rope a couple of turns around his waist and got a firm grip on the loose end with his right hand and on the taut line that angled up to the pulley block with his left hand, and stepped back into the weight. The stone block swung off the ground, and Leoric steadied it as Egwahl backed away from the edge of the hole and raised it higher. Alrys knelt down and reached both hands into the hole and grabbed something and started working it back and forth to loosen it.

The priest lurched to his hands and knees and threw himself into Egwahl's legs, low, near his ankles. Egwahl's feet slipped on the wet

stone, and he let go of the rope. The hemp siz-
zled through the pulley wheels and the stone
dropped straight down onto Alrys' head, driving him into the hole with a crunching splash of
blood and brains. Both of his legs kicked
straight back as his belly hit the floor, and he
spasmed once or twice.

Leoric had danced off balance, trying to
keep his feet out from under the falling stone,
and I reached down and drew my *seax* from the
sheath on the back of Alrys' belt and swung the
blade into the side of Leoric's neck. Blood
sprayed over the floor in a pulsating jet as he
went to his knees, both hands on his neck trying to hold the wound together. The blade had
severed the muscles and tendons to the spine;
his head lolled to the left, and he lost consciousness as he dropped to the floor.

Egwahl was tangled in the rope, which had
spun him around in mid-air like a top when his
feet left the floor and dropped him on top of
the priest, who had lost consciousness again.
Before Egwahl could get to his feet I jumped
over Alrys' legs and brought the *seax* down. He
raised his arm to ward off my blow, but the
blade took his arm off just below the elbow, and
he screamed and grabbed the stump. My next
swing split his skull.

The church was quiet again. I slumped down
on the stacked pavers and put my back against
the stone wall. The place was starting to smell
like blood and shite. Whatever was in the bottom of the hole was still under the stone that
had been quarried and cut by the boys in the

Sixth Legion, cushioned now by a layer of splintered bone and jellied brain. I looked over at the skull Leoric had dug up, its empty eye sockets taking in the scene.

All I'd wanted to do was get in out of the rain and be alone with my thoughts of Oswith, and now I had this mess to clean up. Or did I? The priest was out cold and the others were dead. No one in the village had come to investigate the activity in the church, keeping to their warm houses in the cold rain of *Winterfylleth*.

I went over to where the contents of my bag were scattered on the floor and put them back in the leather satchel, and then stripped my sheath off Alrys' belt, wiped the blade, and slid my *seax* back into the leather. I buckled my belt around my tunic again. The pooling blood looked black in the shadows and the flickering red light from the tallow candles.

Down in the bottom of the hole, Þunor was getting his first drink of sacrificial blood in a hundred and sixty winters. I imagined that after all that time listening to *ceorls* sing off-key hymns at mass he was parched. The gold coin lay on the pavement, a glittering spot in the spreading pool of blood. I picked it up. On one side there was a man's face, and on the other side the words EDWIN REX. It looked as if it had been minted early last week instead of early in the last century, which meant it had found its way into the floor of the church not long after Edwin had turned his back on Wōden, Tīw, and Þunor in favor of the nailed Christ.

Maybe Coifi himself had dropped the coin in the ground, burying the old gods with a token, not quite ready to renounce the beliefs of a lifetime despite a prudent and politic reevaluation of his spiritual priorities.

I searched each of the dead men and found some cut coins and fragments of hack silver and, in Alrys' belt bag, the soft leather pouch that contained the amber-headed cloak pin Oswith had given me. I transferred it all to my belt bag, and I stood up and kicked Alrys' corpse solidly in the ribs.

"That's for the priest," I said. "And for stealing my cloak pin."

I put up my hood and wrapped up in my cloak. There was nothing more to do in the church. The *masse-thegn* would either wake up or he wouldn't, and there was no leechcraft I could offer him that would make a difference. Whatever was at the bottom of the hole was under that heavy stone and what was left of Alrys' flattened head—I had neither the time nor the inclination to satisfy my curiosity about the origin of the gold coin. I stepped over to the door and cracked it slowly and looked outside in case there were any other men waiting in the rain, but I saw no one.

So much for a quiet afternoon spent talking to the ghost of my dead wife and meditating on the ephemeral nature of life; now I had to tramp the rest of the way to Beoferléa in the rain. I'd be walking all night; I wanted to put as much distance between myself and this mess as I could before the sun came up and someone discovered what had happened. If the *masse-thegn* survived, maybe he would forget all about me, and this carnage would be attributed to the swift and terrible agency of the curse that guarded the place. Maybe they'd be right.

I took one last look at the bodies on the floor, and then, like a sparrow, I slipped quickly and quietly back into the storm.

If you have enjoyed this book, please go to its Amazon book page and leave a short review. It will be most appreciated!

OTHER BOOKS BY THIS AUTHOR:

THE ELF-SHOT BOY (780 AD)
[ISBN: 978-1-940469-20-1]

The Elf-Shot Boy is a story about a boy named Ælfgar (Gar) who has what we now call Down syndrome. Just before the midsummer assembly, when boys Gar's age become legal adults, symbolized by getting an iron weapon, a girl called Oshild is raped and murdered. Everyone thinks Gar is too simple to become a legal adult, but he takes it upon himself to help Hring, the assistant advocate in town for the assembly, investigate the crime. What they discover apparently implicates Oshild in the theft of a charter that proves ownership of a nearby estate, which is being contested at the midsummer *gemót*. The more they investigate, the stronger the connection between the murder and the theft becomes. This promises to cause trouble for everyone, but all Gar is concerned about is avenging Oshild's murder and getting his iron.

THE *FRITH* SEAT (783 AD)
[ISBN: 978-1-940469-22-5]

People are being murdered in Eoforwic. That doesn't mean much to Hring, recently an assistant advocate in Elmet, and currently a drunk who's grieving the loss of his wife. When he's falsely accused of murder, he seeks refuge in the frith seat in the cathedral, where he has 40 days to make his peace with God—who he's not sure he believes in anymore—before facing his unjust punishment. For Hring, it's 40 days he can use to hunt down the real killer.

BEWEDDIAN (783-84 AD)
[ISBN: 978-1-940469-21-8]

You can pick your friends, but you can't pick your family; as far as your family goes, you just have to make the best of it. Hring's misanthropic brother Mæl, who operates a grist mill for the kindred, unmarried at the advanced age of 34, has fallen in love with the equally difficult daughter of a neighboring kindred, and no one is in favor of the match. They've picked each other, and they're resolved not to let anything stand in the way: not the objections of their families, not the disharmony between different branches of Mæl's kindred, not even a wedding gift with an agenda of its own.

THE DEEPEST SEA (796 AD)
[ISBN: 978-1-940469-24-9]

This is Charles Barnitz' cult classic. Bran Snorrison, aspiring *skaald* in the Norse town of Clontarf, becomes entangled in a situation involving the sister of his friend and lord, and the son of the local Irish chieftain. Caught between his duty and his growing attraction to a woman beyond his station and financial resources, he goes on his first *vik* to make the brideprice in plunder from the Mercians, and to eliminate his rival, if the opportunity presents itself. Unfortunately for Bran, the Norns have something else in mind. He finds himself on an incredible trek across the changing face of the eighth-century world where old magics fight for life against the new Christian ways.

ABOUT THE AUTHOR

Charles Barnitz is an accomplished author whose who has published stories in *The Denver Quarterly* and *The Madison Review* and had a chapter of his novel, *Mummers*, anthologized in the *Signet Classic Book of Contemporary American Short Stories*. His cult favorite, *The Deepest Sea*, has been released in a new 20th Anniversary edition by **BLOOD AND THUNDER PRESS**. Many of his stories are set in the 8th-century and follow Hring, former monk, now serving as an assistant advocate in the *gemót* courts of the Mercian province of Elmet. Hring is out to see balance restored, even if it takes a little creative interpretation of the law to bring the guilty men to the rope.

Visit Charles Barnitz at:

www.bloodandthunderpress.com